NEW YORK REVIEW BOOKS
CLASSICS

YOUNG ONCE

PATRICK MODIANO was born in the Boulogne-Billancourt suburb of Paris near the end of the Nazi occupation of France. He studied at the Lycée Henri-IV and the Sorbonne. As a teenager he took geometry lessons with the writer Raymond Queneau, who would play a key role in his development. He has written more than thirty works of fiction, including novels, children's books, and the screenplay for Louis Malle's film *Lacombe, Lucien*. In 2014, Modiano won the Nobel Prize in Literature.

DAMION SEARLS has translated many classic twentieth-century writers, including Marcel Proust, Rainer Maria Rilke, Elfriede Jelinek, Christa Wolf, Hans Keilson, and Hermann Hesse. For NYRB Classics, he edited Henry David Thoreau's *The Journal: 1837–1861* and has translated Nescio, Nietzsche, Robert Walser, Alfred Döblin, and André Gide. He is currently writing a book about Hermann Rorschach and the cultural history of the Rorschach test.

YOUNG ONCE

PATRICK MODIANO

Translated from the French by
DAMION SEARLS

NEW YORK REVIEW BOOKS

New York

THIS IS A NEW YORK REVIEW BOOK
PUBLISHED BY THE NEW YORK REVIEW OF BOOKS
435 Hudson Street, New York, NY 10014
www.nyrb.com

Originally published in French as *Une jeunesse.*

Library of Congress Cataloging-in-Publication Data
Names: Modiano, Patrick, 1945– author. | Searls, Damion, translator.
Title: Young once / Patrick Modiano ; translated by Damion Searls.
Other titles: Jeunesse. English
Description: New York : New York Review Books, 2016. | Series: New York
  Review Books Classics
Identifiers: LCCN 2015039565 (print) | LCCN 2015045712 (ebook) | ISBN
  9781590179550 (paperback) | ISBN 9781590179567 (epub)
Subjects: | BISAC: FICTION / Psychological. | FICTION / Coming of Age. |
  FICTION / Literary.
Classification: LCC PQ2673.O3 J4813 2016 (print) | LCC PQ2673.O3 (ebook) |
  DDC 843/.914—dc23
LC record available at http://lccn.loc.gov/2015039565

ISBN 978-1-59017-955-0
Available as an electronic book; ISBN 978-1-59017-956-7

Printed in the United States of America on acid-free paper.
10 9 8 7 6 5 4 3 2 1

For Rudy
For Zina
For Marie

THE CHILDREN are playing in the garden. Soon it will be time for the daily chess game.

"He's getting his cast off tomorrow morning," Odile says.

She and Louis are sitting on the deck of the chalet and watching from afar as their daughter and son run across the lawn with Viterdo's three children. Their son is five, with a cast on his left arm, but it doesn't seem to bother him.

"How long has it been?" Louis asks.

"Almost a month."

He had slipped off a swing, and it had been almost a week before they realized he had a fracture.

"I'm going to take my bath," Odile says.

She goes upstairs to the second floor. When she gets back, they will start their chess game. He hears the bathwater running.

On the other side of the road, behind the row of pine trees, the funicular terminal looks like a spa's little train station. One of the first cable cars built in France, apparently. Louis follows it with his eyes as it slowly climbs the slope of the Foraz, and the vivid red of its cabin cuts into the green of the summery mountainside. The children had dodged around the pines and now they are riding their bikes on the shady roundabout next to the terminal.

Yesterday, Louis had taken a large wooden plaque off the

3

outside of the chalet, the one on which he had written, in white letters, SUNNY HOME. It lay on the ground behind the French window. It was twelve years ago that they bought the chalet and turned it into a kids' camp, and they had not known what to call it. Odile wanted a French name—Les Lutins, Les Diablerets—but Louis thought an English name was classier and would attract more customers. They ended up going with Sunny Home.

He picks up the wooden sign. Sunny Home. He'll put it away in a drawer soon. He feels relieved. The children's home, that's over now. Starting tomorrow, they will have the chalet for themselves. He'll turn the shed at the far end of the garden into a restaurant and teahouse where people can stop in during the winter, before taking the funicular.

Darkness rises up, little by little, from the bottom of the valley and the far end of the garden, along with the screams and laughter of the children now playing hide and seek. Tomorrow, June 23, is Odile's thirty-fifth birthday. And next month it will be his turn: He will be turning thirty-five as well. He'd invited the Viterdos and their children to the chalet for Odile's birthday, as well as Allard, the old skier who runs a small sports store.

The red funicular has started down the mountainside and it disappears behind a mass of pine trees, then reappears, following its path at the same calm speed. They will see it climb back up and descend back down until nine p.m.; the last time, it will be nothing but a fat firefly sliding along the face of the Foraz.

"Don't be scared, my boy."

The doctor patted the child's cheek. Odile was the one

who was nervous. The doctor, with a device spinning as fast as a circular saw used for cutting logs, started to split open the cast where Odile had drawn flowers. And the boy's arm suddenly appeared, intact. The skin was not dry or pale, as Odile had feared. The boy moved his arm, bent it gently, not really believing it, a watchful smile on his lips.

"Now you can go break it again," the doctor had said.

She had promised him an ice cream before they went back up to the chalet, and they sat down face to face at an outdoor café by the lake. The child chose pistachio-strawberry.

"Are you glad you don't have your cast anymore?"

He didn't answer. He ate his ice cream, his face serious with concentration.

She looked at him and wondered if he would remember, later, that cast dotted with flowers. His first memory of childhood? He squinted in the sun. The mist was blowing away on the lake and it was her thirty-fifth birthday. And soon Louis would be thirty-five too. Could anything new happen to them, at thirty-five? She wondered, thinking about the intact skin on the boy's arm suddenly appearing from under the cast; it was like the arm was what had broken open the hard shell they had encased it in. Does life ever start over at thirty-five? A serious question, which made her smile. She would have to ask Louis. She had the feeling that the answer was no. You reach a zone of total calm and the paddleboat glides all by itself across a lake like the one stretching out before her. And the children grow up. They leave you.

An eyelash at the corner of her eye was bothering her and she reached into her bag for an empty compact she kept solely for its little round mirror. She couldn't get the lash, and she scrutinized her face. It hadn't changed. She had the same face as when she was twenty. The tiny wrinkles at the corners of her mouth hadn't been there back then, but the rest was the same, yes...And Louis had not changed either. He was a little thinner, that's all...

"Happy birthday, Mama."

He said it stumbling over the words, but with a certain pride. She hugged him. How strange it would be if children knew their parents the way they were before the children were born, when they were not yet parents but simply themselves. Her childhood, with her grandmother in Paris, on rue Charles-Cros, where the bus lines started. A little farther on, the gray building of the Tourelles swimming pool, the movie theater, the slope of boulevard Sérurier. With a little imagination, that hill on misty, sunny mornings was a steep cliffside road, leading down to the ocean.

"We have to go home now."

Driving the car on the road up to the chalet, her son sitting next to her, Odile hummed a tune, something or other, without thinking about it. Before long, she realized that it was the first bars of an operetta she had found, to her great surprise, at a used-record store in Geneva: *Hawaii Rose*...

They are sitting on the green bench in front of the funicular terminal, and their son is riding his bicycle around the roundabout. It has training wheels. Odile is stretched out with her head on Louis's knee, reading a movie magazine.

The child moves through the patches of sunlight one by one, then restarts what he calls his "grand tour." He stops every so often to pick up a pinecone. The cable-car operator is smoking a cigarette in the doorway to the building, and he looks like a stationmaster with his blue cap and uniform.

"So, how's it going?" Louis says.

"Not many customers today."

It didn't matter. Even empty, the red funicular would leave on schedule. That was the rule.

"Even though it's sunny," the operator says.

"It's not holiday time yet," Louis says. "Just wait, in two weeks…"

The child circles the roundabout and pedals harder and harder. Odile has put on her sunglasses and is flipping through the magazine, holding the pages tight because of the wind.

In his sleep, he hears the children's shouts getting closer and farther away and closer again, and for him this corresponds to the intensities of the different lights, the plays of shadow and sunlight. But he always has the same dream. He is sitting in an empty velodrome, in a seat at the very top, watching his father clutch the handlebars and cycle slowly around the track.

Someone says his name and he opens his eyes. His daughter is standing in front of him, smiling at him. She is almost as tall as Odile.

"Papa…The guests are here."

She is wearing a red dress and that surprises Louis. She is thirteen years old. He is just coming out of his dream and, still drowsy, he is surprised that his daughter could be so tall.

"Papa…"

She gives him a reproachful smile, takes him by the

hand, and tries to pull him off the sofa. Louis resists. After a moment he lets himself be dragged upright, stands up, and kisses her on the forehead. He goes out onto the deck. It's not dark yet and he sees, through the row of pine trees, a group coming up to the chalet. He recognizes Allard's deep voice and Martine Viterdo's laugh. Over there, the red cable car glides slowly along the slope of the Foraz, a lady-bug in the grass.

All the lights in the dining room have been turned off. Louis, Odile, Viterdo and his wife, Allard, and the children are waiting around the table. Louis's daughter comes out of the kitchen carrying the cake, with eight candles shining on it: three for the decades, five for the years. She walks toward them and they sing, in English: "*Happy Birthday to you ...*"

She puts the tray down in the middle of the table. Everyone takes turns giving Odile a kiss.

"Well," Viterdo says, "what's it like being thirty-five?"

"I'm almost old enough to be a grandmother," Odile answers.

"Don't be silly, Odile."

"You have to blow out the candles, Mama."

Odile leans over the cake and blows.

"First try!"

They clap and someone turns the lights back on.

"A song! A song!"

"Odile will now sing for you 'La Chanson des rues,'" Louis says.

"No, no. No way."

She cuts the cake. The children have left the table and all five of them are standing in a group at the edge of the deck. Odile and Louis bring them each a piece of cake on a little napkin.

"They won't want to go to sleep," says Martine, Viterdo's wife.

"It doesn't matter. This is a special day," Allard says in his deep voice. "You don't turn thirty-five every day."

Viterdo checks his watch.

"I think we have to go, Louis. I'm very sorry for the inconvenience."

He has to take the night train to Paris, the 11:03, and Louis has offered to drive him to the station.

"Let's go," Louis says.

Allard, Viterdo's wife, and Odile are sitting on the deck, chatting. Allard's voice dominates the conversation. The night is warm and there's the sound of a storm brewing, far away.

Viterdo, standing in the middle of the living room, opens his black briefcase. He seems to be checking that he hasn't forgotten anything in the rush. The children are bustling on the stairs and the noise of their hurried footsteps fades as they cross the large upstairs rooms. Odile has left the deck and rejoined Louis just when he is about to follow Viterdo out of the chalet.

"Happy birthday," Louis says.

"Oh, enough already," Odile says.

"What's it like being thirty-five?"

She shakes him by the shoulder. "Enough already. It'll be your turn soon too."

He hugs her to him and they burst out laughing. This is

the first time in their life that they are celebrating one of their birthdays. It's a silly thing to do, but maybe the children will like it . . .

Viterdo puts his bag and black briefcase on the seat in back, then gets in and sits next to Louis.

"I really am sorry, Louis."

"It's nothing. Really. We'll be at the station in five minutes."

Louis pulls out slowly. After a moment, he turns off the engine and the car travels down the straight little road in silence.

"When are you coming back?" Louis asks.

"Next weekend. I want to spend August here with Martine and the kids. You get to stay here in the mountains all year."

"I don't think I could live in Paris," Louis says.

He grabs the knob on the radio and turns it on, the way he always does when he's driving.

"How long have you lived here?" Viterdo asks.

"Thirteen years."

"It's barely six years since we bought our place . . ."

"I feel like you've been here longer."

Viterdo is the same age as Louis. He works at an import-export business in Paris. Every year, at Christmas and Easter, he and Martine come to go skiing with their three children, whom they often leave with Odile and Louis so that they can play with the other kids at Sunny Home.

"So, you're done with the home?"

"We're done," Louis says with a smile. "Now we'll have

the chalet all to ourselves. The kids will be able to roller-skate in the rooms."

"And you, what are you going to do now?"

"Maybe start a restaurant and teahouse for the cable-car people, with Allard."

"You're doing the right thing, really," Viterdo says. "I wish I could drop everything and live out here too."

The first turn in the road. To the left, the wall surrounding the Hotel Royal. Louis restarts the car's engine.

"The kids are definitely happier here than they'd be in Paris," he says. "What I want is for my son to become a ski instructor."

"Really? What about your daughter?"

"Oh, you never know with girls."

He has rolled down the window. The storm seems to be moving in.

"Did you ever live in Paris?" Viterdo asks.

"Yes. It was a long time ago."

He stops the car outside the station, opens the door, and picks up Viterdo's bags.

"Louis, please."

They cross the small, empty station hall, lit by fluorescent lights. Viterdo slips his ticket into the machine that stamps it.

"They're more and more complicated, these machines," Louis says. "Luckily, I don't travel anymore."

The train is already in the station.

"Bye, Louis. See you Friday."

Louis walks him to the platform and helps him stow his bag and black briefcase in the sleeping-car compartment. Viterdo, smiling, opens the window and leans out.

"Til Friday, then. I'm leaving Martine and the children in your hands. Be strict..."

"Very strict, same as always."

Crossing the station hall again, Louis notices a candy machine next to the closed ticket counters. He puts two coins into the slot. Something falls down, wrapped in red and gold paper—one of those chocolates called *rochers*, rocks. Huh, they still have those... Odile used to buy them all the time at the bakery on rue Caulaincourt. This would be his birthday present for her.

On the other side of the square, behind the café windows, several motionless silhouettes face a TV screen. The voice of a singer reaches him. Only the voice, a little husky, he can't understand the words. A warm wind starts blowing. On the road back, the first drops of rain...

It rained for days on end in Saint-Lô, that fall fifteen years ago, making large puddles in the barracks yard. He had accidentally stepped in the middle of one and felt an icy shackle grip his ankles.

His tin suitcase in his hand, he saluted the orderly. When he reached the street corner, he could not help turning around to look back at this brownish building that would never again be any part of his life.

His civilian clothes—a gray flannel suit—pinched his armpits and were too tight around his thighs. He would need a winter coat and, especially, shoes. Yes. Shoes with thick crepe soles.

Brossier had said they should meet at the Café du Balcon, around seven. The thought suddenly came to him that he had known Brossier for two months; Brossier was lying to him when he'd said he was only passing through Saint-Lô. Why had he extended his stay here, if his "business" was calling him back to Paris?

He had met Brossier for the first time at this same Café du Balcon, when he was killing time until midnight before going back to the barracks. That afternoon, he had walked along the ramparts, then followed the highway out toward the Haras National horse farm and wandered off into an area of shacks to the right. On his way back into the city, he had stopped at the Café du Balcon and sat down, and the mirror next to the bar reflected an image of himself in uniform, with short hair and crossed arms. Brossier was reading a newspaper at a nearby table, and his eyes came to rest on him.

"Bagger a while yet?"

He used slang words that Louis did not always understand.

"How old are you?"

"Twenty next July."

They were the only customers in the café, and Brossier said with a shrug that the streets of Saint-Lô were deserted at this hour.

"If you can even call them streets."

He suddenly gave a bitter smile.

"It must be no fun, ending up a bagger here, hmm?"

Brossier's age? Forty, barely. When he smiled he looked younger. Blond hair, very pale eyes, flushed skin. He doubtless owed that coloring, and the chubbiness of his face, to a weakness for Belgian beers.

He lived in Paris, he explained, but was spending a few days with his family in Saint-Lô, where his elder brother owned a notary public office. He had not been back here for more than ten years and people had forgotten about him. Anyway, he was using his holiday to put his affairs in order. A guy from Cherbourg wanted to sell him a whole batch of American equipment: old jeeps, old army trucks. Brossier worked "in cars." He even ran a garage in Paris.

That night, he had walked Louis back to his barracks. He was wearing a raincoat and an old Tyrolean hat with a reddish-yellow feather stuck in it. And as they walked down the street lined with new buildings, every one the same gray concrete, Brossier told him, as though sharing a secret, that he no longer recognized the city of his childhood. They had built a new city after the bombardments of the last war, and Saint-Lô wasn't Saint-Lô anymore.

At the Café du Balcon, the cigarette smoke and the noise of the conversations made his head spin. Cocktail hour. He quickly caught sight of Brossier with his Tyrolean hat. He went over to him, slightly uncomfortably, put his bag down, and took a seat.

"So? Demobbed?" Brossier asked him, beaming.

"Yup, demobbed," he said in an undertone, since using military slang had always embarrassed him.

"Any demob's a party, old boy," Brossier said. "Look, I've already gotten started."

He pointed to his glass, half filled with a red liqueur.

"What'll you have?"

The man's patter was like a traveling salesman's, but then his gutteral voice would suddenly turn affected. When he brought up furniture and books. He would explain that he used to work for several antique dealers in Paris. One night, he sententiously listed for Louis the ways you could tell a

Regency armchair from a Louis XV, and even showed him, pencil in hand, what to look for to judge the quality of the backs and arms. As for books, well, he liked first editions. At these moments, Brossier was no longer himself; he was wholly under someone else's influence and doubtless repeating his words and gestures.

"Here's to your demob!" Brossier said after the waiter brought their Camparis.

They clinked glasses and drank. He did not have the courage to tell Brossier that his shoes were soaked.

"What are you thinking about, Louis?"

He was thinking about just one thing: Taking off his sodden socks and shoes, throwing them in the garbage, and being absolutely certain that he would never have wet feet again, thanks to his new crepe-soled shoes.

"What a pain!" he blurted out.

"What, old boy?"

He had been obedient for two years, behaved well, put up with the barracks, the quarters, the uniform, the leaky shoes, and now that it was over he had no idea how he'd been able to stand it.

"I need new shoes."

"All right..."

"Shoes with thick crepe soles."

Brossier looked surprised. He gulped down what was left of his Campari.

"Sure," he said, "let's go find some."

They left the Café du Balcon and walked back down to the commercial street to the right. A row of shops, one after another, under cement arcades. In the last window, they saw moccasins and women's shoes on display. The shopkeeper was just lowering the metal grate.

In the shop's little showroom, they sat down next to each other, Brossier still wearing his Tyrolean hat.

"They're for the young man here," he said.

"I'd like a pair of shoes with crepe soles."

The shopkeeper explained that they didn't have many of those left, but he could show him a "range" of Italian moccasins, the best quality.

"No. Crepe soles."

He decided on the ankle boots with crepe soles more than an inch thick. To try them on, he took off his soaking wet socks.

"You don't have a pair of socks, do you?" he asked.

"Yes, tennis socks."

"It doesn't matter."

He pulled them on and conscientiously tied the laces of the new shoes. Brossier took out his wallet and paid. The shopkeeper handed Louis a package containing his old shoes and wet socks in a plastic bag.

Outside, he threw the package in the gutter, and this ceremonious gesture marked the end of a phase of his life. He still needed a coat, of course, but that could wait.

"Let's have dinner at Neuvotel," Brossier said to him. "I've reserved a table. And two rooms."

"With bath?"

"Yes. Why?"

A private bathroom—it was incredible, after the long sink in the barracks like a trough in a pigsty, with the drains always blocked. A bathroom, after two years of squat toilets with badly fitted doors banging in the icy wind of the courtyard . . .

"That means I can take a bath?"

"As many baths as you want, old boy."

The rain was falling again, but so fine it barely wet his hair. They followed the street's gently curving slope along the ramparts.

"It's funny," Brossier said, pointing out to him a place on the ramparts. "One time, when I was kid, I climbed down from up there on a knotted rope ... So how are your shoes?"

"Great."

A few hundred meters to the Neuvotel. They passed the Drakkar cinema, at the end of the street, before crossing the bridge over the Vire. But Louis didn't mind a long walk, and he felt a certain pleasure in putting his feet down right in the middle of all the puddles. There was nothing, and no one, to fear with these crepe soles.

Soft music was coming from a loudspeaker. The hotel dining room was deserted, except for him and Brossier at a table in the back. Brossier was just opening a bottle of Burgundy when the waiter offered them the cheese plate.

"And here's to demob!" he shouted for the third time, filling Louis's glass.

Louis, already annoyed by this word that kept reminding him of the barracks, ignored the toast. He let himself sink into a pleasant torpor.

"You have to have a '*nègre blanc*' for dessert," Brossier advised. "A *nègre blanc*."

He'd had too much to drink. His face started to turn a scarlet color.

"Tell me, Louis. You wouldn't be in the mood to ..." He turned his head to look around him, then said, in a low voice, "I called for two Cherbourg girls to come, to celebrate your demob."

Louis squinted in the too-bright light. He tried to remember the name of the song coming out of the loudspeaker, a tune you heard a lot of in those days, but he couldn't. What was it called, what was it?

"Two *nègres blancs*!"

Brossier looked around again.

"You know, that's what they're like, Cherbourg girls..."

They were waiting in the lobby. Two brunettes, one with her hair in a ponytail. The car they had come in was hers, a Citroën DS-19 that had almost broken down near Valognes. That would have been no fun in this weather.

"The main thing," Brossier proclaimed, "is that you're here, my dears."

He stroked the cheek of one of the brunettes, who smiled at him. Then he walked over to the reception desk. Louis stayed where he was, his bag in his hand, with the two girls.

"So, it looks like you've finished your military service?" asked the one with the ponytail.

"Yes. It's over."

"Are you going to stay here, in Saint-Lô?"

"Yes."

"I think it would be better to be in the navy. Get to travel..."

The other girl had taken a compact out of her handbag and was putting on lipstick. Brossier came back.

"Let's go! Room 119! Forward march!"

On the narrow staircase, Brossier kissed the girl with the ponytail and started to grope her. She had taken his feathered green hat off his head and put it on her head, askew. Louis, pressed up against the other girl, could only carry his bag in his arms.

A room with deep blue wallpaper, furnished with twin beds and a light wood dresser. A radio built into each of the night tables. Brossier turned the knob.

"Let's get champagne! But first, they'll show you one of their numbers! They have a nightclub act in Cherbourg."

"What's your name?" asked the girl who was still wearing Brossier's feathered hat.

"Louis."

Brossier had turned off the overhead lights. The only light was from one of the bedside lamps. Louis watched the rain come down outside the window, harder than before.

"Three cheers for demob! Three cheers for demob! Three cheers for demob!" Brossier sang.

"Three cheers for demob," one of the brunettes softly repeated.

There was a huge parking lot in front of the hotel, like an airport runway. Two rows of streetlights gave off a garish light. Why all those streetlights? Louis noticed, in the middle of the empty lot, the two brunettes' DS-19.

On the stairs, the vibrations from the drums and electric guitars always overwhelmed Georges Bellune. He sat on the leather bench on the second floor, his back straight, trying to gather his strength before crossing the Palladium's threshold.

Light from the milky white platform area in the back, on the left, where a group of musicians were rocking and rolling, pierced the semidarkness. The singer was belting out an American hit in a voice even more confident than the original singer's. Boys and girls, most of them not yet twenty, crowded around the stage. The band's drummer, with his curly blond hair and fat cheeks, looked to Bellune like a prematurely aged army brat.

Bellune beat a path to the bar and ordered a drink. After the third glass, he was less sensitive to the noise. Every time he came to the Palladium, it took an hour for the bands and the singers to perform onstage, one after the other—teen-agers from the neighborhood, mostly, or young working people. Their dream was so strong, their desire to escape with the music in which they had a presentiment of their lives was so powerful, that Bellune often thought the shriek-ing guitars and hoarse screaming voices he heard were like cries for help.

He was over fifty and worked for a record company. They sent him to the Palladium two or three times a week to scout out various amateur bands. Bellune set up appoint-ments for them at the record company's office, where they would audition. In those moments, he was nothing but a customs officer picking two or three people out of a mass of emigrants crowding in front of a ship and shoving them up the gangway.

He looked at his watch and decided that he had shown his face long enough. This time, he didn't have the strength to pay attention to one more band or singer. To elbow his way up to the stage felt like a superhuman effort. No. Not tonight.

That was when he noticed her. He hadn't seen her be-fore, his back was turned. Chestnut-brown hair, unusually pale skin, pale eyes. Barely twenty. She was sitting at the bar but looking toward the stage in back, hypnotized. A stir went through the room, there was a rush, applause, screams. Someone climbed onstage: Vince Taylor. Why wasn't she up there with the others? Her gaze, fixed on the only zone of light in the Palladium, called up in Bellune's mind the image of a hesitant moth drawn to a lamp. On the platform, Vince Taylor was waiting for the applause and screams to die down. He adjusted the mic and started singing.

"And you, do you sing too?"

She jumped as though he had suddenly yanked her out of her dream, and turned to face him.

"Are you here because you're interested in music?" Bellune asked again.

His gentle voice and serious air always inspired confidence. She nodded yes.

"That's good timing," Bellune said. "I work for a record company. I'd like to help you, if you want."

She looked at him, taken aback. The people Bellune had always chosen for auditions, at random, had at least gotten up onstage and made some kind of noises with their drums and guitars; their faces had appeared in bright light for a moment. But tonight, Bellune chose someone who didn't say anything, didn't move, and seemed drowned in the sea of noise. A face barely different from the shadows.

He took her home in a taxi. Before leaving her there, he wrote his office's address and phone number on a scrap of paper.

"You can call and come see me whenever you want. By the way, what's your name?"

"Odile."

"Odile, good. See you soon, I hope."

She crossed the courtyard of her red brick apartment building at Porte Champerret. In the elevator, she pressed the button for the sixth floor, the highest it went, and when she got there she climbed another little flight of stairs and walked down a hallway.

It was an attic room with a sloping roof. You could just barely stand between the sink and the bed. Photographs of singers—a black woman, an American man—were stuck to the beige wall. The radiator, its size disproportionate to the cramped dimensions of the room, gave off too much heat.

She opened the window, from which you could see, at the horizon, the top of the Arc de Triomphe. She dropped onto the bed and took out of her raincoat pocket the piece of paper where he had scribbled:

Georges Bellune
21, rue de Berri, 3rd floor
ÉLYsées-0015

She would call him tomorrow. If she waited too long, she would lose courage.

The guy seemed serious. Maybe he would help her. She didn't take her eyes off the scrap of paper; she wanted to convince herself that the name and address were really written there.

She had forgotten to buy anything to eat, but there was almost nothing left from her last paycheck anyway. Now that she no longer worked at the perfumery on rue Vignon, she spent almost all her time at the Palladium, like someone lingering in the bath.

She put on a record she found on the floor at the foot of the bed. Then she turned off the bedside lamp. She listened to the music, stretched out in the darkness, with the square of the window in front of her a little bit lighter. Since the crank for adjusting the radiator was missing, it was impossible to lower the heat, and she always left both sides of the double window wide open.

At Gare Saint-Lazare, it was night and Brossier had fallen asleep. Louis tapped him on the shoulder. They waited in their compartment for all the other travelers to leave. Then Brossier put on his old Tyrolean hat, standing in front of the mirror, while Louis took the bags down from the overhead racks: his little tin suitcase and Brossier's garnet-colored leather bag.

There was a long line of people at the taxi stand, and Brossier suggested that they have a glass of something. They went back up rue d'Amsterdam. Louis carried the bags and let Brossier lead the way. He decided on a café whose glass surfaces, at the intersection of two streets, jutted out like the prow of a ship. Harsh light inside. Someone playing a game of pinball. They sat down at the counter.

"Two beers," Brossier ordered, without asking Louis. "Belgian, if you have any."

He took off his Tyrolean hat and put it on a stool next to him. Louis watched the people sliding past the windows like underwater shadows along the surfaces of a bathyscaphe, and looked at the gridlocked traffic at the intersection.

"To your health, Louis!" Brossier said, raising his glass. "Are you glad to be in Paris?"

She would walk down the hall, followed by the sounds of conversations and ringing telephones. People came and went, slamming the doors. A deep calm reigned in Bellune's office, and if you stopped outside the door for a few seconds, you might think that no one was inside. There was not the least sound of a voice. Not even the clicking of a typewriter.

Bellune, standing in front of the sash window, would be smoking a cigarette. Or else sitting on the arm of one of the leather armchairs, listening to a song on a tape player. He would ask her what she thought of it, but the music and the voice would be almost too soft for her to hear a thing. One afternoon, she even surprised him pensively watching the tape unroll without finding it necessary to turn the sound on.

He had worked for the same record company for a long time and, since his role was to "discover"—in his words— "new and exceptional talents," he promised to help her cut a record. But he seemed bored in his office. Every time she came to see him he said, in the same impatient tone of voice, "What do you say we go downstairs, Odile?"

He would take the telephone that never rang off its hook and, in the corridor, turn the key in his office door. Taking her by the arm, he would lead her to the elevator.

They would walk back up the rue de Berri toward the Champs-Élysées, he never saying a word, she not daring to disturb his reverie. Then, in a very soft voice, he would tell her the time had come for her to make a tape they could present to the record company. He had to find some good songs and he would ask a few songwriters he knew. Some "classic things," going against the tide of what "the young people" were singing nowadays.

He would fall silent once again and, as they walked back down the street in the other direction, she would have the feeling that he had suddenly lost interest in her, maybe even forgotten she was there. She would ask him a timid question about the record but he wouldn't answer. He would stare straight ahead: "It's a hard business...very hard."

He would say it so indifferently that she would wonder if this business still interested him at all.

They would arrive back at the door to number 21. Just before entering the building, he would make a plan to see her that evening.

"See you soon, Odile."

She would linger a few seconds, hesitating, wanting to go upstairs and surprise him again, like the time when the tape was spinning in the tape player. Maybe he spent his afternoons like that, watching black bands of tape unspool in silence.

The hotel Brossier had chosen for him, before leaving again for another "business trip," was located at the far end of the fifteenth arrondissement, on rue de Langeac. One room, with bath; it had a brown wood bed and a piece of paper on the wall with mauve flowers painted on it. A woman of uncertain age, with short hair, brought him up a plate of breakfast at around nine o'clock. He ate every bit, even the sugar cubes and whatever was left of the jam after spreading the rest of it on his bread. During the day, he might order a sandwich at a café counter. He had calculated that with the hundred and fifty francs Brossier had loaned him, he would last more than a week this way. By that time, Brossier would surely be back from his "business trip" and would introduce him—as he had promised—to "the important friend of mine who will give you a job."

Ever since the interminable days he had spent in the barracks infirmary, he'd had the habit of listening to his transistor radio in its green leather case. Lying down, looking at the ceiling, he would think about the future, or in other words about nothing, while listening to the news bulletins, songs, and quiz shows, one after the other. He smoked a cigarette from time to time but tried to make the pack last, because they were expensive, these cigarettes. English, they came in metal boxes. The others had made fun of him for it back in the barracks, but he didn't like brown tobacco.

At the end of the afternoon, he would leave the hotel with his room key in his pocket, after casting a furtive glance at the glass door to reception. The bald man with a tanned face was playing chess; all he could see of the man's opponent was his back. Outside, he turned onto rue de la Croix-Nivert. The restaurant was far uphill, and often, along the way, he would stop at Saint-Lambert Square. There, on a bench, he would wait until dinnertime, smoking a cigarette. Brossier had given him an old gabardine coat and a tweed jacket, which came in handy: Winter that year started early and very cold, and then, with the snow, the temperature dropped even further.

The restaurant looked a bit like a dining hall because of the large tables for eight or ten, each with a label stating the name of the waiter or waitress responsible for it. He would sit at the "Gisèle" table. For nine francs, he would get an appetizer, a main dish of meat and vegetables, a dessert, and as much table wine as he wanted. A fresco ran around the walls, showing a Savoy landscape—the province where the restaurant's owner was from.

He would exchange a few polite words with the people next to him, mostly men, some of them locals, others taxi drivers. He'd have a coffee, happy to linger in the midst of all these people, in the smoke and the kitchen smells that permeated their clothes. Rue de la Croix-Nivert. At night, he would walk all the way to boulevard de Grenelle.

At the intersection, under the elevated Métro bridge, music from a loudspeaker would be smothered by the din of bumper cars. He would stop for a moment beside the track, to watch the poles sliding along the ceiling, leaving a trail of sparks, and the pink, apple green, and purple cars. Then he would keep walking, along the median, down to the Seine.

Later, when Roland de Bejardy told him about his father, he remembered the constriction in his heart every time he passed the stairs to the Métro station before coming out onto the quai. To the left, there were new apartment buildings on the site of the old Winter Stadium, the Vélodrome d'Hiver, where he knew his father had competed in cycling races. And on the nights when he was working in Bejardy's office and looking through old bound issues of sports magazines to pass the time, gluing the articles that mentioned his father's name among the other Vel' d'Hiv racers into an album, he would see himself standing alone, in front of the apartment buildings that had replaced the velodrome, with the clatter of the Métro over his head and the feeling of being nothing more than a speck of dust in the dust of boulevard de Grenelle. And yet, there was the presence of something in the air.

Bellune's gaze, as he stood at the window, rested on her the moment she crossed the street and stayed on her for several seconds. Then she disappeared into the crowds of the Champs-Élysées.

She walked down the avenue and, since it was starting to

rain, stepped under the Arcades du Lido. A woman leaving a store jostled her; farther on, she passed a man who smiled at her. He turned around, followed her, and approached her when she left the gallery.

"Are you alone? Do you want to come have a drink with me?"

She immediately looked away and hurried down the street. The man tried to catch up to her but stopped under the entrance to the Lido. She walked farther, and he didn't let her out of his sight, as though he had made a bet he could keep her in sight for as long as possible. Small groups of people came out of a movie theater. He could still see her chestnut-brown hair and the back of her raincoat, and before long she had blended in with the others.

She went into the Sinfonia. At that time of day, there were lots of customers. She slipped to the back of the store. She chose a record and gave it to the salesman so he could let her listen to it. She waited for one of the booths to be free and sat down, putting the little headphones over her ears. A silence like cotton wool. She forgot the hustle and bustle around her. Now she lets the singer's voice envelop her, and she closes her eyes. She dreams that one day she will no longer walk around in this crowd, in this suffocating racket. One day, she will burst through this screen of noise and indifference and be nothing but a voice, a clear voice, set free, like the one she is listening to at this moment.

At the Iéna Métro exit, she walked down the street to the Seine along the Trocadéro gardens. Bellune lived a little farther down, on one of the streets perpendicular to the Quai de Passy.

The apartment, on the top floor, had a deck upstairs from which you could see the roofs of the neighborhood, the Seine, and the Eiffel Tower. Bellune had arranged chairs and a table along the edge of the deck, by a white banister like a ship's railing.

The living-room windows looked out onto the street and the furniture consisted of a long table, a leather armchair, and an upright piano. A hallway led to Bellune's room. On the left wall of the hall, there was a little poster the size of a playbill, on which it said:

HAWAII ROSE
BY
GEORG BLUENE
with
GUSTI HORBER
AND
OSCAR HAWELKA

The letters of the title were interwoven with garlands of roses. Above the title was a medallion containing a photograph of a dark and handsome young man, in which she recognized Bellune.

"Is that you?"

He didn't answer. The next day, they were eating dinner in the restaurant on Square de l'Alboni—they always had dinner in a neighborhood restaurant, as if Bellune was afraid to stray too far from where he lived—and he gave her a partial explanation. At twenty-three, when he still lived in Austria, he had written the music for that operetta, a huge success in Vienna, where he was born, and then in Berlin too. But as bad luck would have it, the launch of his career coincided with the Nazis' arrival in power. A few years later, he'd had to leave Austria for France, and he had never written music again. He made do with working in radio and then for the record company. He described it all indifferently, as though it had happened to someone other than him.

After dinner, he would sometimes take her to a club where amateurs were performing. Bellune would be disappointed by the acts but, to satisfy his conscience, he would stay to the end. One night, at a place empty of customers near the Sacré-Coeur—on rue du Chevalier-de-la-Barre, to be exact: the street had an intriguing name—the show was performed for just the two of them. Under dim lights, a singer with bleached-blond hair wearing a sky-blue suit was throttling his electric guitar while bobbing his head up and down. Bellune, impassive, kept his eyes fixed on him. Then a little brunette in a white lace dress started to sing a lullaby. Between each number, a presenter, with the air of an absentminded street vendor, tossed out a few witty remarks. A tall girl with a bulging forehead, her face and bust like the figurehead of a ship, interpreted some sea shanties. And then it was a chubby, grinning woman's turn; she performed a string of long-winded jokes. The light turned orange, opal, turquoise, and Bellune congratulated the artists. The evening made a deep impression on Odile.

It must have been from watching him surreptitiously under the lights, and finding him mysterious, even handsome, like the young man in the medallion, the one who had written, in Vienna, the music for *Hawaii Rose*.

She ended up wondering what would happen to her without him and feeling lost whenever he was not by her side.

One night, when she was going to Bellune's apartment later than usual, policemen were stopping cars and checking drivers' and passengers' IDs. She saw them from a distance but didn't dare tell the taxi driver to let her out so she could avoid them.

At a uniformed man's gesture, the taxi pulled over to the sidewalk. She rummaged in her bag for her passport and handed it through the lowered window.

"You're a minor..."

The agent made a sign for her to get out. She paid the fare, and the taxi driver indifferently handed back her change, without even turning around.

The police van was parked a little farther away, in the side alley off boulevard Berthier. They pushed her inside.

"A minor."

"How old?"

"Nineteen."

Inside, there were two men in uniform and a fat blond man in civilian clothes. He examined her passport.

"Do you live with your parents?"

"No."

"Are you a student?"

"No."

The door slammed shut; the driver turned the van around and took boulevard Berthier. She was wedged between the two uniformed cops. The fat blond man, sitting on the bench across from her, looked at her and casually waved her passport back and forth like a fan.

"What are you doing out at this hour?"

She didn't answer. Anyway, he had asked the question in a tired voice, purely for form's sake. He did not seem interested in the answer.

"Stop on rue Le Châtelier a second," he told the driver.

He slipped the passport into his jacket pocket. The police van made a right turn into a little street, slowed, and stopped.

The fat blond stood up and got out. Since he didn't shut the van door behind him, she saw him go into one of the buildings through a glass and wrought-iron door. On the wall, a lit sign said: GOURGAUD RESIDENCE.

For a brief moment she thought about trying to escape. One of the uniformed policemen had gotten out of the van too and was pacing up and down the sidewalk. The other was sitting on the bench across from her and had closed his eyes. But how could she get her passport back? The cop on the sidewalk would stop her anyway.

Suddenly she felt tired. The two windows on the ground floor of the Gourgaud Residence were lit and she could see through the left one a green plant whose large leaves stuck to the window like suction cups.

"You want a cigarette?"

The cop held out his packet. She said no.

"Do you think they'll keep me here a long time?"

"I don't know."

He had shrugged his shoulders. He was young, twenty-five at most, and seemed tired. He sucked on his cigarette in a sly, shifty way, holding it pinched it between his thumb and index finger.

The fat blond came out of the Gourgaud Residence with another man, very tall, with a cane. The cop in uniform who was pacing outside climbed back into the van at once, as though he had to leave them alone together, and sat down next to her. The two men on the sidewalk were talking in very loud voices and occasionally burst out laughing. She could hear scraps of their conversation. It was about someone named Paul.

They continued their discussion, sometimes drifting away from the van, and she wondered every time if they were going to come back. Maybe they had forgotten about her? The two policemen, for their part, dozed off. The fat blond man and the other man came back to the van again, talking very loud.

She thought it would go on all night and that she should go to sleep like the two cops. But the blond man leaned in through the van door.

"You can get out."

The other man was standing a few feet away, leaning on his cane.

"I'm not going to give you back your passport now. You'll have to come get it tomorrow, at two o'clock. Understand?"

He told her the address of the police station in the seventeenth arrondissement.

She walked straight ahead, without daring to turn around, sure that the two men were staring at her back. When she reached avenue de Villiers, she heard the sound of the police van's engine as it hurtled past her.

A café was still open at place de la Porte-Champerret and she wanted to phone Bellune and tell him everything, but she didn't have the courage to ask the cashier for a token.

A gap in the line of buildings: boulevard Bineau. She was at a flat open area at the edge of the city.

All it would take would be to walk down the boulevard, through the gap, toward Neuilly, and it would be like pulling herself up out of a swamp and reaching the open air.

But she went left, crossed the courtyard of the large

apartment complex, and walked up the stairs. In her room, she stretched out on the bed and fell asleep at once, without even getting undressed or turning the bedside lamp off.

Louis woke up with a start. Someone was knocking on the door to his room very loudly.

"Rise and shine! It's Brossier. I'll wait downstairs."

He got dressed quickly and went downstairs without even combing his hair. Brossier was leaning on the front desk.

"Let me take you to breakfast."

It was still dark out. Barely seven o'clock. They walked into a café on rue de Vaugirard, where the waiter was just finishing putting the chairs on the floor around the tables.

Brossier dipped his buttered toast in the café au lait and gulped it down with a voracity that surprised Louis. He was wearing a new hat that was the same kind as the old one, with the same reddish feather stuck in it. His coat looked new, too: loden, like the hat.

"Not bad, this coat, hmm? You need one like this... You'd look great. I'll take you to Tunmer's. You can't wear my old gabardine forever... Sorry to get you up so early, but I'm leaving again, for five days... To the southwest... I'll arrange things for you when I get back."

He slipped some bills folded in four into Louis's hand.

"Here's your pocket money. And don't forget, when I get back you'll start work. I'll introduce you to that friend I told you about..."

He looked at his watch and seemed preoccupied.

"If you want to reach me, you can leave a message at Hotel Muguet, rue Chevert, in the seventh. They'll give it to me. Hotel Muguet... INValides-0593."

He wrote the phone number down on a piece of paper.

"Let's plan to meet up in five days, at the same time, at the Alcyon de Breteuil on avenue Duquesne."

What could he be going to buy or sell in the southwest? Louis wondered. Tires maybe? The idea made him want to laugh. Yes, tires.

"You worked for a year at Paris Perfume, on rue Vignon?" the fat blond asked.

"Yes."

"Why aren't you working there anymore?"

She lowered her head, and noticed that her stockings had a run.

"I called them. It was nice of them not to press charges. Then again, shoplifting a few tubes of lipstick at your age, it's not so terrible. No, no... Don't worry..." His voice had become soft and gentle. "Did you know that your mother had a file back then?"

A file. What did that mean? He handed her a sheet of paper with her first and last name written on it, her date of birth, and the words "Father unknown." Below that, her mother's first and last name. She read phrases at random: "The party was living by her wits... affairs... black market... Pacheco's mistress during the German occupation... Questioned by the department, Quai de Gesvres, September 1944... Deceased in Casablanca (Morocco), February 14, 1947, thirty-two years of age..."

"We have a good memory."

He propped his elbows on the black plastic typewriter cover and smiled kindly at her. But she found his smile frightening, and the run in her stockings seemed to her like a wound that kept her from fleeing the room.

"Your move," the fat blond said.

She crossed the hall of the railway station and went into one of the waiting rooms. Empty. She sat down and started flipping through a magazine, trying to soothe her nerves.

After a while, people started to come in and sit down. It was rush hour. The commuter trains unloaded their passengers while the crowds of people who had spent their day working in Paris pushed onto the departure platforms. This inverting of the hourglass would last until eight at night.

It would be easy to lose herself in this mass of people, to escape the surveillance of the fat blond man and the other two, and get on a train, it didn't matter which. But one of the plainclothes policemen came into the waiting room, sat down next to the door, and buried his nose in a newspaper, paying no attention to her.

Before long, all the seats were full. She looked around, keeping her eyes off the policeman. Exhausted faces, people waiting for their trains. A woman gave off a smell of face powder that mixed with the smell of cold tobacco. On the back wall, there was a white and sky-blue colored poster, with a skier gliding alone in the middle of a huge expanse of snow that reflected the sunlight. And the words: HOLIDAYS IN THE ENGADINE.

A man outside the waiting room pressed his forehead

against the glass door. Would she ever get out of this aquarium? Someone next to her stood up and left the room. The man looked at her through the glass. After hesitating a moment, he came in and sat down in the empty seat, and the edge of his coat brushed against her knee.

"Do you have the time?"

His voice, high and squeaky, didn't go with his square face and crew-cut hair. He was wearing a bow tie.

Before answering him, she glanced quickly at the plainclothes policeman, who gave her an almost imperceptible nod.

"What train are you waiting for?" the man asked her.

"The train to Cherbourg, at nine."

"Me too. What a coincidence. Would you like to have a drink while we wait? It's almost an hour."

His voice was getting more and more high-pitched, but he also had a strange way of forming his words, as though his mouth were covered in vaseline.

"If you want . . ."

He walked fast, without letting her out of his sight. The plainclothes policeman followed them at a distance, off to one side.

"Let's have a cup of tea away from the station. I know a quiet place . . ."

It was dark. He opened a car door. A DS-19. Then, in a sharp tone: "The place isn't far, but it'd be quicker to drive."

He drove down rue d'Amsterdam.

"You're . . . a student?"

"Yes."

"What do you study?"

She didn't know what to answer.

"English."

His hands on the wheel. A bit pudgy, and white, and entirely hairless. He was wearing a wedding ring. Before sitting down in his car, he had taken his coat off and folded it carefully. His suit was navy blue, his bow tie gray.

He took rue Saint-Lazare and looked from side to side.

"Funny, this neighborhood . . . I don't like this neighborhood." His lips pursed.

"Look at that. Disgusting."

A woman was waiting under the rue de Budapest arcade and, behind her, a group of men were standing by a hotel's front door.

"Don't you think that's disgusting?"

Since she didn't answer: "You realize, if you were a girl like that . . . Disgusting, isn't it?"

He turned onto rue de Londres.

"They take all comers. Poor girls . . ."

"Is it far, where you're taking me?"

"No. It's right here. Poor girls."

She decided to get away at the next red light. Suddenly he turned left into a small, deserted, very narrow alley that looked like a private driveway. He stopped. She tried to open the door but it was locked.

"Wait a minute, I want to show you something . . ."

She anxiously pushed the door handle again and hit the window with her shoulder.

"No, no. Don't bother, I have the key."

He turned around and placed a black briefcase on the backseat. He opened it and took out a large brown leather-bound album, then put the briefcase away again.

"Here, look."

He opened the album. Carefully glued onto its pages

were the kind of "special" photographs that twins with red, pockmarked faces used to peddle on the sly on boulevard de Clichy. He turned the pages carefully, with one finger, as though they were the pages of a missal.

"Look … This one … is … my favorite …"

A woman in a black velvet eye mask, in profile, was sucking a faceless man's penis.

"Do you like her?"

He had let go of the album. He grabbed the back of her neck. She struggled but he held her tighter and tighter. He pinned her to the back of the seat with his right shoulder, reached back with his left arm, and opened the glove compartment.

"Wait … I have to take my precautions …"

He held up a half-unrolled condom, a few inches from her face.

"You don't mind, do you? I'm afraid of diseases."

He gripped her tighter and tighter and she tried to get free. He pushed her down onto the seat and she felt his whole weight on top of her.

"It won't last long. Don't move …"

All she could see was his gray bow tie, beating against her eyes.

"Don't move … It'll be quick …"

But one of the car doors opened. Someone pulled the man out of the car by his jacket collar. She sat up and the fat blond man helped her get out.

They had shoved the man against a wall, between two high, locked shutters, and as he gesticulated wildly one of the plainclothes policemen was slapping him over and over with the back of his hand. They dragged him to their car, parked at the entrance to the alleyway.

"I'll be right there," the fat blond shouted as the other two pushed the man into the car.

Then, looking a little embarrassed, he went up to her.

"That's that. We can go have a drink, if you want."

The door of the DS-19 was still open. He closed it, after picking up something from the backseat.

"He forgot this."

The fat blond showed her the bow tie, then shoved it in his pocket.

They sat down at a table in a nearby café, on rue de Londres.

"Two kirs!" the fat blond ordered.

She drank hers down in one gulp.

"Have another."

He had taken the bow tie out of his pocket and, while he fidgeted with it, told her about the man that he and his colleagues had just apprehended, "thanks to her cooperation." An engineer, from Bois-Colombes. It had taken three months to track him down ... He had almost killed a young German girl like that, the bastard.

She was hardly listening, still upset by what had just happened. And the two kirs in a row she had drunk made her light-headed.

"Another kir? Sure, come on. I'll have another too."

He knew it would end at Gare Saint-Lazare. From long experience, going back to when he'd started with the force in this neighborhood. Saint-Lazare was the lowest place in Paris, a pit, a kind of sinkhole. Everything slips down into it eventually. You just have to wait. Once they were swimming around in the swamp of Saint-Lazare, you could hook them like a pike. It had been proven true again.

"Tomorrow you'll give a deposition. They'll throw the book at that nut and I'll give you back your passport."

He stood up, heavily.

"Same address, all right? For the deposition. Tomorrow, two o'clock, at the Galvani police station. Then you can forget this ever happened."

He gave a vague smile and left the café in one smooth stride. He had forgotten the bow tie on the table, and she couldn't take her eyes off it.

In the end, what had happened didn't matter at all. She wouldn't even tell Bellune about it. She ordered another kir. Someone behind her was playing pinball and she heard the voice of a singer she liked, someone all the jukeboxes were playing that year, a flat voice, muffled, neither a man's nor a woman's, soaked up by the smoke, the jingling of the pinball machines, the murmurs of conversation, the splutter of the coffee machines, and the night on the square outside where the windows of the Royal Trinité Hotel glittered.

Only one thing mattered. They would give her back her passport.

Finally, one afternoon in his office on rue de Berri, Bellune introduced her to two men: an obese, almost bald man with a black briefcase in his hand, and another with curly blond hair and hollow cheeks. Berne and Sardy, songwriters. They had written four songs for her and Bellune handed them the music-publishing contract, which they signed.

During the whole following week, she learned the songs with an Austrian pianist Bellune had known back at the time of *Hawaii Rose*, whom he sometimes used as a kind of secretary. When she knew the songs well, Bellune chose a date for the recording session.

He went with her into the studio. She recorded the songs in two afternoons. Then he had several test records pressed with her four songs on them, "flexi-discs" as they were called. That night, she listened to them at his apartment, and she could hardly believe that when she put the disc on the record player, the voice she heard was her own. Bellune encouraged her, saying over and over that her voice on it sounded perfect, her contract was practically signed already. One of the songs was called "The Birds Return"; the chorus of another song began: "I threw my heart into the waves."

He had wanted to bring in one of the flexi-discs with her songs himself, and she was waiting for him near the record company, in a little street running alongside the Gaumont Palace.

When he returned, he told her that "the wheels were turning" and that he would definitely get a positive response back within a week. Then she could sign the contract.

He decided to go back to his office on foot and they walked down boulevard des Batignolles on the sunny side of the street. Bellune said nothing and seemed preoccupied. She asked him lots of questions, which he didn't answer. Eventually she asked him if there was something worrying him.

"No, not at all. Nothing."

They turned left at the corner, onto boulevard Malesherbes, and Bellune, glancing distractedly at the buildings, suddenly stopped in front of a tiny town house whose door and one single window made it look like a dollhouse.

"Look. How funny."

His slight accent, which was never really noticeable except when he spoke her name—Odile—was suddenly thicker. She stood next to him and looked at the building too, without understanding what it could be that had so struck him.

"It's so funny. Do you know what it was, back then? The Austrian consulate general."

"Really?"

"Yes. The Austrian consulate general . . ."

He was lost in his memories. With a very gentle gesture he put his hand on her shoulder and said, as if talking to a child, "One day, I reported to this building. The first year I lived in Paris. Austria already no longer existed. But there was still an Austrian consulate general."

He lowered his voice, the same way you read *Sophie's Misfortunes* to a little girl in a conspiratorial tone of voice, to enthrall her more.

"So I walked into this building, which was the Austrian consulate. And they told me I had lost my Austrian nationality. The end. No more passport either. So I went to Parc Monceau and sat down on a bench."

He took her by the arm and, after one last look at the building's black façade, pulled her toward the park gate.

They sat down on a bench, near a sandbox where children were playing. He didn't seem to want to go back to his office right away.

"We should stay outside in the sun for a bit."

"Yes, good idea, Odile."

The story he had started to tell her seemed a little vague to her, and she would have liked him to give her more details, but he leaned his head back on the bench and, eyes closed, offered his face to the sun. She would have liked to know, for example, if he had sat on this same bench that afternoon, back then, after his visit to the consulate general of an Austria that no longer existed.

She rang the buzzer several times in a row. Nobody home. Since she had a key to the apartment, she opened the door herself.

She called out but he didn't answer. The apartment was silent. Bellune must have stayed late at the office.

There was a large envelope on the table in the living room, with her name written on it in red pen. She opened it. It contained the rest of the flexi-discs of her two songs and a letter.

> My dear Odile,
>
> By the time you read this, I will have ended my life in a room at Hotel Rovaro, avenue des Ternes. I have lived in that hotel for a long time. I had just come from Austria. But it would take too long to explain and I don't want to bore you.
>
> I'm optimistic about your record. Go see Dauvenne or Wohlfsohn for me, ÉTOile 50-52. They'll help you.
>
> With love, and, as it says in a song from my youth, *Sag' beim Abschied leise "Servus."*
>
> Georg
>
> Don't stay in the apartment, they might bother you with all kinds of questions.

She didn't have the strength to stand up, and she couldn't take her eyes off the piano, where a ray of sun lit up part of the keyboard. She thought about the afternoons by the piano with the old Austrian, Bellune's sometime secretary, who taught her the songs and even played her the overture to *Hawaii Rose* for fun. She stayed sitting in the leather armchair with the large envelope in her hand.

The telephone rang but she didn't move. The ringing went on for a long time, then, in the silence, the ray of sunlight slid along the gray carpeting.

The phone rang again. This time, she went over and picked up.

"Hello?"

"Who's this?"

It was a man's voice, nervous.

"A . . . a friend of Monsieur Bellune's."

"Wait. Hold on, please."

The man was talking to someone. She heard a murmur of voices.

"Hello, is this Georges Bellune's residence?"

A more muffled voice than the first. She hung up. She used to walk past the Trocadéro gardens. The same way every evening, for two months. The gardens. The quay. The arch of the Bir-Hakeim bridge. She remembered the Trocadéro's aquarium, which she had gone to see with him, and the stairs they had taken to get back up onto boulevard Delessert. He had remarked that the neighborhood was built on several levels, on a hillside, which was what gave it its particular charm. And the nights on the deck, those remarkably mild December nights after the snow had fallen—nights when they would try to penetrate the mysteries of the windows and rooftops they could see nearby.

She asked to see a phone book in a café and looked up the hotel's address, then walked up avenue des Ternes.

When she reached the right number, she saw an ambulance and a police car parked on the sidewalk and several uniformed policemen talking to each other. They were gathered in front of the entrance to the hotel. Two men came down the stairs and she quickly turned away. She had recognized one of them: the fat blond from the other time, the one who had used her as bait in Gare Saint-Lazare. The previous week, she had gone to the Galvani police station to sign the deposition, and he had given her back her passport.

She ran, without daring to look back, afraid of seeing that the fat blond man really was following her, like those shimmering blue flies you can't get free of, that cling to your face or your hands. She was sure that if it was him lurking around there, it meant Bellune was really dead.

She sat at a café table in the passageway connecting Gare Saint-Lazare with the Hotel Terminus. She looked out the window, down at the street and the people leaving the station and waiting at the taxi stand. A vague idea of taking the train, leaving Paris as fast as she could, had guided her steps here, and she remembered the fat blond's remark: In the end you always wash up in Gare Saint-Lazare, at the bottom of the pit.

It was dark. A monotonous coming and going between

the concourse and the café. People gulping down a drink in a hurry and leaving to catch their commuter trains. Down below, they tumbled into the taxis by ones and twos but the line at the stand never got any shorter. She alone was motionless in the middle of all this restless activity.

She ordered a kir, the same as the other time with the fat blond man. She forgot why she was there. Her head was spinning from the people sitting down, getting up, sitting down, from the din of the concourse. How long had it been since she had slept? She no longer saw anything around her except blurry silhouettes, big moving blotches, while insects buzzing around her ear drowned out little by little all the other sounds.

Brossier had lowered the window of his compartment and leaned his head out.

"I'll call you at Hotel Langeac the day after tomorrow, Louis. Around five."

The train shuddered into motion. Brossier, leaning out the window, gestured urgently: five fingers of one hand. It clearly meant: "Don't forget, five o'clock."

Louis walked back to the concourse. It was too late to go have dinner at rue de la Croix-Nivert. He was heading for the stairs out of the station when he noticed, to his left, the little café in the glass passageway. He went in, sat down, and ordered a café au lait and two pieces of bread.

There were no other customers this late. Except one girl at a table in back who seemed to be asleep, her forehead resting on her folded arms. Louis saw only her brown hair.

The light in the cafeteria was a slightly murky yellow, as though used up, dirtied, by the breath of everyone who had breathed there during rush hour. The only bright, clear light was coming from the dark window next door, where a poster was stuck to the wall: HOLIDAYS IN THE ENGA-DINE.

The whole time he was eating his bread, he couldn't take his eyes off that hair spilling over the table. A neck, a forehead, a hand were barely visible. Not the least movement, the least sign of breathing. Maybe she was dead.

He drank his coffee. The waiter had left and now a silence reigned, barely disturbed by the sounds of the diesel engines of the taxis parked in front of the station, or the regular slamming of the doors. On the table, next to the girl's hair, was a glass half full of something; Louis wondered from the color if it might be a grenadine.

The waiter reappeared and started to put the chairs up on the tables. It was closing time. Louis paid his bill.

"Is she asleep?"

The waiter pointed at the girl collapsed on the table. After hesitating a moment, he went over and shook her shoulder. She slowly looked up.

"We're closing!"

She blinked and squinted, not understanding. Louis was struck by how pale she was. She rummaged around in her pocket and took out some coins, which she put on the table. The waiter counted them.

"You're three francs short."

She rummaged in her pocket again, with a hunted look, but couldn't find anything. Louis stood up and put a five-franc bill on the table.

"Thank you."

The concourse was deserted. Louis followed her. She was walking slower and slower, and he was afraid she might fall.

Finally, she sat down on a bench, next to the ticket windows.

"Are you all right?" Louis said.

"I don't feel so good . . . I'm afraid I might faint."

He sat down next to her.

"Do you want some help?"

"Thanks. Just sit here a minute. It'll pass . . ."

At the far end of the station, at the tables outside the large restaurant, a group of soldiers on leave were singing, every verse interrupted by shouts or bursts of laughter. A few people were heading toward the departure platforms with the slowness of sleepwalkers. Louis thought back to the crowd that had just been there, when he had accompanied Brossier to the train. After the tide ebbed away, there was no one left in the gigantic empty hall but him, this girl, and the soldiers back there, beached like clumps of seaweed.

He helped her stand up and supported her by the arm. Going downstairs, he felt the pressure of her hand. She was even paler than in the concourse, perhaps because of the fluorescent light. He led her to the taxi stand. Luckily there was no line.

She murmured her address so softly that it was he who had to tell the driver: "Porte Champerret."

She could barely make it up the stairs and he held her arm as they walked down the hallway. She pointed to the door to her room and gave him the key, which he had a hard time turning because you had to put it into the lock only halfway. She fell onto her bed.

"Do you want something to eat?" Louis said.

"No, thank you."

Her face was so pale that he wondered if he should call a doctor.

"I'm feeling better…" She gave him a weak smile. "Can you stay here with me a while? Just until I'm better."

"What's your name?"

"Odile."

He sat down on the edge of the bed. She closed her eyes and opened them again at longer and longer intervals. Soon she was alseep.

Should he go look for something for her to eat or drink? The cafés were surely still open around Porte Champerret. But he risked having her wake up while he was gone. He realized that Brossier had forgotten to give him any money. All he had left were two five-franc notes.

She was sleeping, her left cheek pressed against the pillow. He took off her boots, which had zippers on the side. The room was tiny. You could just barely stand between the sink and the bed. He saw the photos of the singers on the wall and a tear-off calendar above the sink, with January 4 showing. Mechanically, he tore off the pages. It was January 12.

Why was the window wide open? He shut it. The radiator was on much too high and he looked in vain for the crank to adjust it. Aha, he understood and reopened the window.

He was hungry. How would ten francs last for five days? He lay down next to her and turned off the bedside lamp.

Odile looked in all her pockets and pulled together three ten-franc bills and two francs eighty-five cents in coins.

Toward the end of the afternoon, Louis went around the block and bought a liter of milk, some bread, and slices of ham. He called Hotel Muguet, and they told him that Brossier would not be back until next week.

So that they wouldn't suffer too much from hunger, they slept and rested in bed for as long as they could. They lost all notion of time, and if Brossier hadn't come back they would never have left that room, not even the bed, where they listened to music and little by little drifted off. The last thing they saw from the outside world were the snowflakes falling all day on the sill of the open window.

Louis introduced Odile to Brossier, waiting at a table at the Royal Champerret.

"What do you do?" Brossier asked.

"I'm putting out a record."

"A record? Must be a lot of competition these days."

He turned to Louis: "As for him, we're trying to get him a good position. I have hopes that he'll really go far."

He had adopted a fake paternal tone that neither of them liked, and they exchanged a look. Louis was sure she was thinking the same thing as him about Brossier. Meanwhile, Brossier was considering Odile with a look that he no doubt meant to be charming.

"When I was young, I had dreams of a career in the arts too..."

He smiled, about to indulge in a personal story.

"Believe it or not, I met someone who encouraged me back then. A remarkable man. He enrolled me in an acting class... Unfortunately it didn't work out. I looked too much like an actor named Roland Toutain."

He started breathing more slowly, to better impress upon them the importance of his words.

"When it comes right down to it, that's the only thing I really would have liked to do... Well, anyway. Are you two going to live together? It's over there?"

He gestured to the large apartment block across the street.

"Yes. We'll live together," Louis said.

"That's great, at your age. You can live on air, hmm?"

He took off his Tyrolean hat and put it on the table. This one was a darker green than the others, almost blue. He must have had a whole collection.

"At your age, I didn't have a care in the world either. I'll tell you about it someday..."

Odile, who had kept her face impassive until then, started showing signs of impatience. Maybe Brossier noticed. He raised his head abruptly.

"Tell me, Louis. I made plans with my friend Bejardy. Thursday at three. His place...You'll need to shave, old boy. You look like a bum."

The apartment was on Quai Louis-Blériot, in a group of buildings with access from avenue de Versailles as well. When they got to the fourth floor, Louis noticed, next to the doorbell, a little marble plaque with gold engraved letters on it: "R. de B."

"What does that mean?" he asked Brossier.

"Roland de Bejardy."

Brossier rang the bell. A man opened the door: brown hair, tall, around forty.

"Roland, let me introduce Louis Memling... Roland de Bejardy."

"Nice to meet you."

He led them into the living room, a spacious room whose windows looked out over the Seine. After indicating a light blue velvet sofa for them, he sat down behind a Louis XV desk.

"How old are you?"

"He's twenty," Brossier said, without giving Louis a chance to answer.

"That's good."

Bejardy gave him a protective, patronizing look. There was no paper on the desk, nothing but a telephone. But there were piles of folders sitting on the sky-blue carpet.

"Graduated high school?" Bejardy asked.

"No."

"He just finished his military service," Brossier said.

"Anyway, a diploma..."

And Bejardy swept the back of his hand across his desk. The way he sat there, with his energetic face, regular features, wavy brown hair, back held straight, broad chest in a Prince of Wales jacket, he seemed like a successful lawyer, and the words "star lawyer" came to Louis's mind. Maybe because of the magnificent piece of furniture he was sitting behind, definitely because of his deep voice.

"You've already told him about the kind of work I'd like to give him, yes?"

"Not yet."

"All right. It's not complicated. It's a night watchman's job, in a garage. Now when I say 'night watchman,' in fact, it's more of a job as a...secretary...You'll have to answer the phone, open the door for clients..."

"What do you think, Louis?" Brossier asked.

"I'll take it."

"Good, you can start right away," Bejardy said.

So the man wasn't a "star lawyer" after all, as appearances had led him to believe. The word "garage," like a false note coming from his mouth, came as a shock to Louis. He had to make a mental effort to see this man as the manager of a garage.

"You'll start at . . . fifteen hundred francs a month," Bejardy said.

"All right with you, Louis?"

"Yes."

"Of course there'll be bonuses," Bejardy said.

He stood up and led the others over to the far end of the room. Brossier grabbed Louis's arm and whispered to him, "You see his office, Louis? Purest Louis XV style . . . Look at those bronze moldings, stencil-cut, in the back there . . . acanthus leaves . . ."

They sat down on a different light blue velvet sofa. A plate of appetizers had been set in the middle of the low table, which was black lacquer, with short, turned legs, maybe Chinese.

"Whiskey? Port?"

Bejardy offered them glasses. Louis took a look around. A library covered the wall to the right, with books in massive, flamboyant bindings arranged on the shelves, most of them in slipcases. Across from the library, on the marble mantelpiece, was a photograph of a beautiful young brunette in a silver frame. Bejardy's wife? Was this guy really a garage owner? Louis didn't dare ask him.

Through the French window, he could see the quays and the white Citroën factory across the Seine. A crane rose up from the blocks of stone. What did it mean that here was this extremely luxurious apartment of Bejardy's, and there, on the other bank, that landscape of factories, docks, and warehouses under a gray sky? No, Bejardy didn't live here by chance, and he must have felt the contrast between the book bindings and overly heavy carpet in the living room, and the sad little houses in Javel.

"Is your name really Memling?" Bejardy asked.

"Yes."

"Are you related, by any chance, to Memling the bicycle racer? The one who married a dancer at the Bal Tabarin?"

Louis hesitated a moment.

"Yes. We're related."

Curious about the place where his mother had worked, he looked up the Bal Tabarin's address, but at its number on rue Victor-Massé he found himself in front of a blind façade. They must have turned the old music hall into a dance hall or a garage. It was the same feeling as the one he'd had the night he walked down boulevard de Grenelle for the first time to contemplate the Vel' d'Hiv, in memory of his father.

So neither of the two places that had been the center of gravity of his parents' life existed anymore. A feeling of anxiety rooted him to the spot. Sections of walls were falling on his mother and father, in slow motion, and their interminable collapse raised clouds of dust that smothered him.

That night, he dreamed that Paris was a black cross with only two places lit up: the Vel' d'Hiv and the Bal Tabarin. Panic-stricken moths flew for a moment around the lights before falling into the hole. Little by little they formed a thick layer, on which Louis walked, sinking up to his knees. And soon, turned into a moth himself, he was siphoned up with the rest.

Children played in the courtyard at noon. He heard their shouts and cries through a half sleep. Odile had already left, busy working on her record. He had breakfast across the street at the Royal Champerret, where Odile would come meet him. Later, he would go with her to her appointments. First she was going to the record company behind the Gaumont Palace, to meet with Dauvenne or Wohlfsohn, as Bellune had advised her to. It was Wohlfson who met her there.

He listened to the end to the flexi-disc and told her, in a very gentle voice, that "it wasn't right for their list" but that he would give her a list of impresarios, club managers, radio people, and other record company executives who might be interested in "this project." He drew up the list in front of her, occasionally consulting a phone book to check an address or phone number. Then he folded the sheet of paper and put it in an envelope.

"Here you go. I'll also give you my business card. Say that I sent you."

He stood up and walked her to the door of the office. He shook her hand, and said, in a suddenly emotional voice, "Did you know Georges Bellune well?"

"Yes."

"It's really terrible. Such a good person …"

He was still standing in front of her.

"I knew him in Vienna … before the Flood."

She didn't know what he was trying to say. Before the Flood?

"Good luck to you."

He stuck his head out the door and said again, "Good luck."

———

Sometimes, before her appointments, they would sit in the waiting room together. The interview usually didn't last long, and she would come back out looking discouraged, her flexi-disc in her hand.

In the places where he waited alone while she presented her songs, he would flip through the magazines piled on the low tables, like in a dentist's office. There were articles on the new records, the hits du jour, full of names most of which would disappear next season. Busy people opened doors, letting out bursts of music.

One evening, when he was waiting outside, in the middle of a hallway, for her to finish playing her record for someone, Odile's voice came to him, smothered by the clacking of typewriters, the hum of conversations, and the ringing of telephones, and he wondered if there was any point to all this.

They had been sitting in a large lobby for a long time, and they could see through half-open doors the empty offices that their occupants must have just left, leaving behind polluted air and a smell of cigarettes. The clock on the wall across from them said eight o'clock.

"I'll wait for you outside," Louis told her. "I'll be at the café across the street."

Ten past eight. She couldn't take her eyes off the clock, its dazzling glass and steel. The silence in the room was so deep that she could hear the faint crackling of the fluorescent bulbs. She stood up and walked over to one of the windows. Night. Outside, a stream of cars flowed down avenue de la Grande-Armée and the double windows muffled the sound of their engines. On the other side of the avenue was the café where Louis was waiting for her. Would she have the strength to go back to him? It was raining.

"Monsieur Vietti will see you now."

She followed the secretary down a white-walled corridor harshly lit by fluorescent lights, like the waiting room. The secretary pushed open a leather-padded door and let her in.

Two men were in the room, on either side of a semicircular wooden desk. One of them stood up. Tanned skin, fringed suede jacket. He headed to the door. Odile, who had recognized him, greeted him shyly. He answered with a smile.

"Goodbye, Frank," said the man who had stayed behind the desk.

"Bye."

After he had left the room, the other waved Odile over to the desk.

"Hello."

"Hello," said Odile, her voice filled with nervous excitement.

"Yes, that was Frank Alamo," the man said, as though answering a question she was about to ask. "I like his work very much. Especially 'Allô Mademoiselle.'"

Brown hair, very young, tan like Frank Alamo, whom he resembled a little; dressed in a navy blue pinstripe suit, even a tiepin. On his desk, which was covered by a sheet of glass, were lots of folders and two telephones.

"Wohlfsohn sent you?"

His soft voice surprised her. Usually the people who occupied officies like his spoke in a domineering voice.

"Would you like to play me your songs? Of course, I'd be delighted to hear them."

He was almost whispering. She took one of the flexi-discs out of her bag.

"You've already recorded them?"

"Yes. There was someone . . . Georges . . . Georges Bellune, who recorded them for me."

"Bellune? The one who—"

A phone call interrupted him.

"No. Don't put anyone through."

He hung up.

"It's sad, Bellune's story. I think he maybe worked here for a while. Did you know him well?"

"Yes."

He had taken the flexi-disc and put it on a record player next to his desk. Then he took her over to a large gray sofa.

"We'll be more comfortable here, while we listen . . ."

Before sitting down next to her, he went over to the leather-padded door and bolted it shut.

The disc had been played so many times that the songs sounded worse and worse to Odile. Her voice was almost inaudible. Bellune had told her once that flexi-discs get worn out fast if you play them too much. Like life, he had added.

She dreaded the moment when the record would stop. She would have to stand up and say goodbye, as usual. She felt that she was worn out too. She let herself sink into the silence and the comfort of this pale-colored office: gray carpet, light wood, gauze curtains reaching the bottom of the bay windows, blue lampshade.

"They're nice, your songs. Very nice. Of course it will be a little hard to make a record right away..."

He put his hand on her shoulder and she didn't move. Fine fingers, surely with manicured nails.

"But you could sing them at a club. After that, we'll see. I'll try to set something up tomorrow. That's a promise. After tomorrow..."

He unbuttoned her blouse and she didn't resist. Then she lay on her stomach and he slipped off her skirt and panties and massaged her thighs. She felt disgusted when she remembered his overly well-groomed fingers. She stared straight ahead, her chin on the arm of the sofa. The lights of the avenue looked blurred through the gauze curtains like the contours of the furniture and the things in the room. It was raining outside. Here, at least, she was sheltered from the storm. All she had to do was not move and, as Bellune used to say, in an expression that she particularly liked, melt into the scenery.

Well, if this guy could help her... He smelled of a kind of eau de toilette whose scent remained in her memory, and much later, when she thought back to this time in her life, the smell came back to her along with the memories of her waits in the lobbies of record companies, the subways at rush hour, the station hall at Gare Saint-Lazare, the rain, and the radiator in her room that gave off too much heat because the crank to adjust it was broken off.

The tree-lined street that the garage was on stretched out before Louis like a country lane leading to a château or the edge of a forest. According to Bejardy, no one knew whether the street was in the seventeenth arrondissement, in Neuilly, or in Levallois, and Bejardy liked this lack of clarity.

Louis ate dinner with Odile in a restaurant at Porte de Villiers. Its sign read: À LA MARTINIQUE. Along the walls, on the faience tiles, sparkled a landscape of palm trees, sand, and emerald-colored ocean. Around nine o'clock, he left for his job.

It was not really a garage but a hangar, with an ocher-colored structure rising up beside it, its ground floor accessible directly from the hangar through an iron door. A cement staircase led up to a room on the second floor, narrow but very long. There were rows of glass cabinets along the walls, with files in them, and a magisterial desk presided over the middle of the room. Louis, looking through its drawers, which were mostly empty, had found a few sheets of stationery with the letterhead Paris Automobile Transport Company, rue Delaizement, 9 bis, and an old business card for Roland de Bejardy, 3, avenue Alphand, Paris, 16th arr., KLÉ-08-63. There were two leather armchairs and a sofa, and a telephone on the desk—the old kind, black, on a round base.

What did his work consist of? Opening the hangar doors whenever he heard the bell ring. This required no great physical effort since the doors slid open easily. Someone would drive one of the cars out of the hangar, or else bring back another. On some nights, no one rang the bell at all; on others, there were a lot of comings and goings for him to note down. Always the same faces: a man with brown hair and a mustache; two blond men, one of them with curly hair, a chubby face; a man older than the others, with a crew cut and round steel-rimmed glasses. Others whom Louis paid no attention to. He closed the doors again after they had come or gone. At the desk, he answered the phone, and the voices—maybe they belonged to the men who rang the bell at night—told him on what day and at what time he should expect which car, and Louis wrote the information down in a datebook that he showed to Bejardy later.

At first he was curious and asked questions. Bejardy explained that the business rented out "chauffeured vehicles," but that his other "activities" did not leave him time to manage this one. Louis had noticed that, along with the large American cars, there were often Mercedes of all kinds, and no sooner had someone parked them in the hangar than someone else came to take them out.

As he got used to the routine, he stopped asking questions. It was a night watchman's job and he had to keep himself busy until morning. Bejardy had shown him, in one of the cabinets, some large volumes bound in red leather: a complete collection of issues of a sports magazine. And Louis, leafing through them, had discovered photographs of his father competing in six-day races or sprints. Bejardy had given him permission to cut out the photos. So Louis bought an album to glue the pictures into, in chronological order, as well as every article with the least mention of his father, down to lists of racers in which his name appeared.

Odile would spend the night on the sofa with him, and often they would not answer the phone when it rang. She would bring him something to eat—a sandwich or a bar of chocolate. They made plans for the future. If she ever succeeded in recording an album, or if she got a job in a nightclub, then he wouldn't need to work here anymore. But for now, his night watchman salary was their only source of income.

When he was alone, he cut out photographs and articles, glued them into his album, and wrote down each one's date with a red ballpoint pen. He avoided looking through the magazines from the year in which his father and mother had been killed in a car crash, but he had looked right away at the issue published the week he was born. That night, at the Vel' d'Hiv, after a raucous toot on a horn, the announcer had said that one of the racers, Memling, had just become a father, of a baby boy, and that they were offering a bonus prize of thirty thousand francs in the new baby's name.

She had hardly any time to sing between the Caucasian knife-thrower's act and the entertainer who imitated every kind of birdcall. Vietti—the man with the manicured fingernails—was there the first night. He had told the manager of the Auteuil cabaret-restaurant about her, then taken her back to Porte Champerret at around one in the morning and told her he would record her songs soon, but first she had to "learn the ropes" a little.

Onstage she wore a very large satin skirt and a bolero studded with black beads of jet, a costume she'd borrowed from the manager.

Brossier had told Bejardy about Odile, after Bejardy had questioned Louis one morning, in the garage, on the topic of his "fiancée." And when he heard that Odile was singing in a nightclub, he seemed amused, and decided that they absolutely must go and hear her. He reserved a table for three: himself, Brossier, and Louis.

Bejardy knew the establishment from the old days. According to him, the decor had not changed since then. There were the same dark velvet curtains and the same eighteenth-century-style paintings on all the walls: courtly portraits and amorous scenes.

"You took me here one night with Hélène and your mother," Brossier said to him.

"You think so? We used to come here in the avenue Alphand days."

"No, it was with Hélène and your mother. I couldn't have been much older than you are now, Louis."

Louis wasn't listening to them. He was waiting anxiously for Odile to appear onstage. Up until then, Odile had not let him come see her perform; she was afraid his presence would give her stage fright. But Louis said he had no choice but to come along that night, with the people he called his "bosses."

"It isn't the same clientele though," Bejardy observed, casting a cold look around.

He consulted the menu. Blinis and caviar. Krug champagne. Pierogies while they waited. He didn't ask either Brossier or Louis what they wanted. A palpable authority emanated from his wavy black hair, his high forehead, his straight back and broad chest.

"No, not the same clientele at all."

At the table closest to theirs, some Indonesians were ceremoniously bowing their heads before beginning their meal.

"Are they paying your fiancée well, at least?" Bejardy asked.

"I think so."

Louis, unable to swallow even the smallest bite of food, nervously emptied his glass of champagne.

"Come on, eat," Bejardy said, serving him a blini.

"Louis is nervous for his fiancée's sake," Brossier said.

"Don't worry. I'm sure she'll be wonderful."

The Caucasian dancers bowed, to the jerky sound of

music, and the lights went down. Only a pale blue beam remained, which lit up the center of the stage. Silence. A violin. She appeared in the pale blue ring, a little stiff in her bolero and long satin dress.

"Your fiancée?" Bejardy asked.

"Yes."

She sang. Louis knew the song by heart and was terrified that she would forget a word or abruptly stop. He dug his nails into the palms of his hands and shut his eyes. But her voice remained pure. Odile didn't seem to have any stage fright, and her motionlessness was rather charming, especially at the end, when she sang the old Jean Sablon hit, "La Chanson des rues":

> It speaks to you of sadness,
> Of dreams and loves gone by,
> And of the bygone years that only
> Left you wondering why...

She inclined her chest in a shy bow. The soft clapping from the Indonesians was drowned out by Bejardy's "Bravo! Bravo!" Brossier waved his arm and gestured for her to come join them. She took a seat next to Louis.

"This is Monsieur de Bejardy," Louis told her. "You already know Jean-Claude Brossier."

Bejardy shrugged. "Please, call me Roland."

He bent forward and kissed Odile's hand, and it was unclear whether he meant it with any irony or not.

"I liked your act very much. Especially 'La Chanson des rues.'"

The bird imitator came onstage. The various calls, coos, trills, and chirps unleashed hilarity among the Indonesians. Having sat there so impassively before, they seemed unable to keep their wild laughter under control. They infected Brossier with it.

"Sorry."

"I liked it very much," Bejardy repeated, "and I'm sure you are going to have a wonderful career."

"Me too, me too," Brossier said, between tears of laughter.

The birdcalls became more and more shrill and frantic. Louis started to laugh as well. Odile, too, a nervous laugh. Then the birdcaller fell backward, as though shot through the forehead, and, lying on the ground, arms outstretched, let out an interminable ululation. He suddenly sprang up and disappeared.

"You should have a little champagne," Bejardy said to Odile. "And sing 'La Chanson des rues' for us again."

She drank from Louis's glass. Bejardy ordered another bottle.

"Have you been performing at this club a long time?"

"No, not too long," Odile answered timidly.

"She's going to cut a record," Louis said. "She's here to try out her songs."

Odile gave him a questioning look. How long would they have to sit here with Brossier and Bejardy? Louis answered with a wink, and she smiled.

"I used to know the owner of this club, but he can't possibly still be here," Bejardy said. "You remember, Jean-Claude. A guy who always wore riding pants..."

"The one now doesn't wear riding pants," Odile said.

Louis poured Odile another glass of champagne, and, as if he knew that she hadn't eaten: "You need to eat something. You must be hungry."

"Yes, of course," Bejardy said. "Please, have some blinis."

He summoned the maître d'.

"But first, a toast, to your health," Brossier said to Odile.

"To a singer of great talent," Bejardy said.

They both raised their glasses. Odile looked at them, half curious, half amused, as though observing the frolics of two exotic animals in the zoo. She kicked Louis under the table.

"You're right, Jean-Claude, I remember now," Bejardy said suddenly. "We *were* here with Hélène and my mother..."

At around two in the morning, Bejardy invited them over for a nightcap. They hailed a taxi. During the drive, Odile fell asleep, her head on Louis's shoulder.

Bejardy turned on all the lights in the room where he had received Louis on Louis's first visit, and the sudden, too-bright glare was blinding. Bejardy rolled a drink cart over to them. Louis and Odile politely refused any more alcohol. Brossier and Bejardy poured themselves a little chartreuse.

"This really is a nice drink," Brossier said after taking a sip. "You feel like you're diving into the green . . . You should take a plunge too, Louis."

"A real poet, isn't he?" Bejardy said, turning to Louis and Odile. "You both look exhausted. You can sleep here, I have a guest room for friends. Yes, yes, I'd be happy if you did. It's not a work day today."

He stood up.

"Come with me, I'll take you. Jean-Claude and I will do a little more work. I brought the folders."

"Of course, Roland," Brossier said.

They had bright eyes and the fresh, energetic look of

people who had just gotten a good night's sleep, which surprised Louis.

The bedroom was next to the living room. Its light blue walls, thick carpet, fur bedspread, and the veiled light of a bedside lamp created a gentle, relaxing atmosphere.

"The bathroom is over here . . ."

Bejardy opened a door and turned on the light, revealing a bathroom with blue mosaic walls and floor.

"Good night. You'll be able sleep through the night for once, my dear Louis. And tomorrow, we'll meet at Pointare, one o'clock sharp."

This was a restaurant near the garage, where Bejardy often had lunch.

When he had left the room, they stretched out on the fur bedspread, and as though she did not have the strength to undress herself, Louis took off her shoes, then the rest. They saw their reflection in a large standing mirror.

"Your friends are working some more?" Odile asked.

"Yes."

"What are they doing?"

"I don't really know," Louis said.

They heard Brossier and Bejardy talking in the living room. Later, Louis woke up and heard them still talking, their voices joined by others. He listened to the uninterrupted murmur of conversation and felt himself relax.

Odile slept. Through the window, whose curtains they hadn't drawn, he saw the Seine and the bright building of the Citroën factory on the opposite shore.

Bejardy gave him Saturdays and Sundays off. Brossier was free on weekends, too, and he suggested to Louis that they spend their "moments of leisure" together. He wanted to introduce him and Odile to his fiancée. By getting closer to Brossier, Louis would surely get more information about what had prompted Bejardy to entrust him with a job, and who exactly this Roland de Bejardy was.

He had received his salary the day before and managed to persuade Odile to join him. She would have to show up at the Auteuil cabaret-restaurant at around ten o'clock, and neither she nor Louis understood why Brossier had told them to meet him at the Cité Universitaire Métro station at the start of the afternoon.

The inner pocket of Louis's jacket was bulging with fifteen hundred francs, and Odile would receive her fee after that night's show. They were rich. And it was the first sunny day of the winter. In the train, on the Sceaux line, they felt like they were setting out on a trip.

BROSSIER was waiting for them on the platform at the Cité Universitaire station, as though they had just arrived on holiday and he, their friend, had come to meet their train. Plus, as he came up to them, he said "No luggage?" in a tone that left Louis confused, to the point where he wondered if they were really still in Paris, not at the seaside.

Even Brossier's clothes were disconcerting. Still a Tyrolean hat with a red feather, but no boring, rumpled traveling salesman's suit, no black socks and shoes. No. Instead, a print shirt under a white sweater, linen pants, and white sneakers, a monochrome look that Brossier seemed proud of. He hadn't shaved. Or brushed his hair. Louis and Odile admired this new man. He walked them to the stairs leading out of the station.

"This way, my friends."

They crossed the boulevard, led by Brossier, and entered the Cité campus.

"Here's where I spend my weekends," Brossier said with a smile. "Come with me, it's this way."

They took a path to the left between areas of grass, crossed the threshold of one of the massive buildings, and walked down a hallway, running into groups of students.

"My fiancée is waiting for us in the cafeteria. Here we are."

The cafeteria was deserted at this early-afternoon hour. A beautiful black woman with harmonious Ethiopian features was sitting at a table all the way in the back, and Brossier walked over to her.

"This is Jacqueline, my fiancée. Odile...Louis...Jacqueline Boivin."

She stood up and shook hands with them. She looked a little intimidated; she was around twenty years old and wearing a gray pleated skirt and a beige twinset: conservative clothes that didn't match Brossier's sporty look. He invited them to sit down at the table.

"I recommend the pan bagnats, they're excellent here. Don't you think so, Jacqueline?"

She agreed with an almost imperceptible nod of her head.

Louis and Odile said nothing while Brossier walked over to the counter. They both smiled at Brossier's fiancée without daring to speak, and when Louis offered her a cigarette from his pack, she refused with a furtive gesture. Brossier rejoined them, carrying a tray piled high with pan bagnats that he handed out to them. After taking a bite of his own, he said, "Juicy, aren't they? Maybe you'd like a little harissa to make it spicier? I prefer it without."

And he dug into the roll.

"Yes, Jacqueline is a student, she lives here at Cité Universitaire. As for me..."

He rummaged through his jacket pocket and took out a card that he handed to Louis.

"Look, I managed to get a student ID printed up. You need it to eat at the university cafeteria...and to feel like you belong."

Louis looked at the card. It was in Brossier's name, with

his photograph, and listed a college address. Odile examined it in turn.

"And you sleep here?" she asked bluntly.

"Every weekend."

He liked being able to reveal his secret, and he put his arm around his fiancée's shoulders.

Odile handed him back his student card, which Brossier looked at too. He handled it carefully, even though it was encased in a plastic sheath.

"I made myself a bit younger...Oh, just ten years or so..."

"What exams are you taking this year?" Odile asked.

"The generals in literature. What are they called again, Jacqueline?"

"Propaedeutics," Jacqueline said in a pinched voice.

He pulled her closer, and she rested her head on his shoulder.

"How did you get this card?" Louis asked.

"Bejardy knows someone. A Pole, who made false papers during the war."

He said it unwillingly, as though it was a sore point and he was sad he wasn't a real student.

"Jacqueline is a mathematician, just think...She's taking courses at the Faculty of Sciences."

"Where did you meet?" Odile asked Jacqueline.

"Here, in the cafeteria." She had answered in a slow, soft voice. "I always saw him alone here in the cafeteria. He looked bored. So we started talking."

"Yes, I've been coming here a long time," Brossier said. "Especially when I felt low. I always liked Cité. It's a different world...I would wander around the corridors of all the buildings, sit in the TV rooms. You know what I mean. This place has something about it."

As he was talking, Louis started to see him in a different light. How could he ever have guessed that this man, as chatty and jokey as a guy hawking something on the street, and who, he had told Odile, "dealt in tires," was strolling around in his time off under the shade of the trees at Cité, an Ethiopian on his arm and a fake student ID in his pocket?

"Does Bejardy know?" Louis asked.

"No, not yet, but I'm planning to tell him. Nothing surprises Roland, you know. We'll invite him out here some night. Jacqueline has to meet him."

They left the cafeteria. Brossier wanted them to see the Cité campus and wanted to point out all the various buildings, like the provinces of his kingdom.

"We were just in the Provinces of France building, the most important. I like the England building more, in front of you. It reminds me of a hotel in Aix-les-Bains. Before I met Jacqueline, I often used to spend the evening reading a newspaper in the England building."

He was holding Jacqueline's hand and growing more and more eloquent as they continued their visit. He explained to Odile and Louis that people stayed out late on the great lawn in the summer to listen to the voices and laughter of the night. In June, there was the Cité festival— a ball in the Provinces of France building.

"You have to come see how nice it is here when it's spring…"

He pointed out a building with a steel and glass façade.

"The Cuba building… The Cubans are great. They bring so much joy and excitement to Cité… Tell me, have the two of you ever wanted to be students?"

"You mean a student like you are?" Odile said, bursting out laughing.

A student. That was something that had never once crossed Louis's mind, or Odile's. How could they ever go to university?

"I can get you IDs, if you want."

"I hope you'll keep your promise! Will you?" Odile asked. "I'd like to be a student."

For her, and for Louis, these two syllables had a mysterious harmony: Those who were "students" seemed as distant and incomprehensible to them as members of an Amazonian tribe.

"Everyone here is a student?" Odile asked.

"Yes."

A group of boys and girls were scattered across the lawn and some of them were improvising a volleyball game without a net. Their shouts were in a language that Louis didn't recognize.

"Yugoslavians," Brossier said.

He showed them Grand Café Babel on the boulevard, which was, he said, like a branch of the university. It was so nice to have a drink there on June nights and listen to the leaves rustling in the trees. Then they walked toward Parc Montsouris.

"You see that building there, in the middle of the lawn?" Brossier said. "It's an exact replica of the bey's palace in Tunis."

They sat at an outdoor table at the Chalet du Lac.

"There," Brossier said. "Now you've seen practically our whole kingdom."

And he told Odile and Louis that, if he could, he would live there forever, without feeling the least desire to venture beyond its magic perimeter. Jacqueline, his fiancée, didn't know a thing about Paris outside Cité Universitaire and its Faculty of Sciences.

It was much better that way.

"Don't you think so, Jacqueline?"

She said nothing, happy just to smile and take another sip of her grenadine.

They had dinner very early, in the dining hall. Its size and wood paneling made Brossier feel like he was in the reception hall of an English manor house. Next time, he said, they would have to eat in the other dining hall, which was much more modern, with big bay windows and trees all around so that you felt you were swimming in a sea of green.

"And now," Brossier said, "let's go back to our place."

They walked down a gravel path to the edge of a village. The little houses shaped like bungalows, cottages, and cabins were strewn all across the meadow, among the flower beds and groves of trees.

"This is the nicest spot on campus," Brossier said. "The Deutsch de la Meurthe area."

They had arrived at one of the buildings, a Norman-style house with slanting roofs. A flight of stairs led up one side with a rough-hewn banister. Brossier let the others go first.

"All the way up."

It was a spacious room, with a balcony even. Near the bed, the wall was covered with photos of Jacqueline. No furniture except a cane-back chair.

"Have a seat on the bed," Brossier said.

Jacqueline withdrew to an adjoining bathroom and came out wrapped in nothing but a red bathrobe.

"Sorry," she said. "I feel more comfortable like this."

And she stepped gracefully over to the bed to sit with them.

Brossier handed them tumblers and poured them each a little whiskey. Jacuqeline put a record on the player: a Jamaican song. They didn't talk. Brossier poured them another whiskey. He had taken his sweater off, and Louis contemplated the design printed on his shirt: the sail of a Chinese junk unfolded against a pink sky, with a pagoda visible on the horizon, atop a craggy mountain.

"Now Odile can sing us 'La Chanson des rues,'" Brossier said.

"If you want…"

Louis let himself sink into the listlessness that Odile, Jacqueline, and Brossier were visibly feeling too. Odile had wrapped her arm around his waist and rested her chin in the hollow of his shoulder. She listened to the music with her eyes closed. Brossier caressed Jacqueline's shoulder as she lay next to him, her breasts visible in the neckline of her robe.

It was too bad they couldn't abandon themselves completely to this carefree indolence. Ten o'clock—Odile risked being late to work.

They were sorry to leave. Plans were made to spend next weekend together at Cité. Or why not come back tomorrow, on Sunday, Brossier said.

When they got outside, they looked up. Jacqueline and Brossier were smiling down at them from the balcony. Silence all around them. The smell of moss. They found their way back by the lights of the other buildings. How would they get back to boulevard Jourdan and the station? From the heart of this little village, Paris seemed so far away... In the half dark, Louis could have sworn that they were in a forest clearing.

She was removing her makeup in her little booth off the big room when Vietti came over with the nightclub's manager. They sat down to wait on the sofa in the big room.

"So, your engagement is coming to an end," Vietti said.

"When?"

"Tonight."

She had the strength to give them a smile.

"Yes, that's right," the manager said. "I'm afraid I have to let you go."

Odile's smile vanished.

"It's not you, I have to shorten the show..."

"It's nothing serious," Vietti said.

"Not at all. I'm sure you'll find a new gig very soon."

Neither of them seemed particularly to believe it.

"In any case," the manager said, "you were very good. I'm entirely satisfied with your work, it's just that I have to change the formula of the show. You understand, don't you?"

When she felt the tears rising up to her eyes, she went back into the changing room and shut the door. The men continued talking. She did not turn on the lightbulb and she rested her forehead against the door. She heard the manager's shrill laughter. She stayed in there, in the dark.

"Hey, what are you doing?" Vietti asked.

"Would you like to have a drink with us?" the manager suggested.

She didn't answer. Someone turned the knob to open the door, but she had latched it shut.

"Here. This is for you, the rest of your fee."

The sound of an envelope sliding under the door.

Vietti turned on the radio before he headed out. A jazz tune, which he turned down.

"So are you going to stay locked in that changing room all night? Idiot..." He shrugged. "I have to go back to the office, I forgot something. Do you want to come with?"

She didn't answer. She put her hand in her pocket and squeezed the envelope. She did not have the courage to open it in front of Vietti. She would never sing again, and nothing was left of the dream she had chased for so long except for an envelope, in which they had slipped her "the rest of your fee," as the nightclub manager had said.

"Sulking?" he said in a slightly exasperated tone, and he put his foot on the gas. It was almost one in the morning and he was driving faster and faster down boulevard Suchet, then boulevard Lannes, both empty.

"Still don't feel any better?"

He could drive as fast as he wanted, she didn't care at all.

"You should just run the red lights."

"You're crazy."

And he hurtled into the tunnel under Porte Maillot. He never stopped admiring his Italian sports car; he had even told her, one night, that there were only four people in Paris who had this kind of car, with an Allemano body.

The smell of his cologne nauseated her more than usual, but that too didn't matter. On the contrary, she took a certain pleasure in noticing all the details about his person that repulsed her. His tan, which looked fake even though he had just come back from a ski trip, and the excessive care he took with his clothes: tiepin, vest, a pocket watch he never stopped taking out to look at. His oily, husky voice.

"So, still sulking? I don't like girls who sulk, you know."

He wasn't usually so familiar with her. No mention of the record he wanted her to make. He had never believed in that record, she now knew. He turned up the volume on the radio, bobbing his head with the beat.

"I need money," she said abruptly.

"Money? Are you serious?"

"Two thousand francs. I want you to give it to me."

She herself was surprised at her sudden confidence, but all at once it was like she was not afraid of anyone, as if all her timidity and scruples had disappeared and she was ready for anything.

"I really need those two thousand francs. Tonight."

"Well, we'll see. You'll have to be very nice to me…"

She walked behind Vietti, and the fluorescent lights blinded her, just like the first time, when she was sitting with Louis in the waiting room chairs. The same stagnant smell was in the air.

Vietti turned the key in the leather padded door and sat down behind his desk. She took refuge by the window. The street was empty and the large café opposite, where Louis had waited for her, was still lit. She looked at the lit sign: CAFÉ DES SPORTS. She felt like leaving and calling Louis from the café, to tell him that she would be back right away.

"Well, now you have to earn your money. Two thousand francs, that's a lot, you know. It'll cost you."

He looked through a folder on his desk without raising his eyes to her. Then he took a record out of its cover.

"Here. Now this is a talented girl. My last discovery. You want to listen?"

He put the record on the player.

"Stand in front of me. Take your clothes off."

He said it in an unctuous tone, a smile fixed to his face, like someone posing for a photograph.

"She's really talented, don't you think? You wish you could sing like that? I'm going to get her on Eurovision next year…"

The mischievous voice of a little girl, smothered by electric guitars.

"I'll have to fuck her too, one of these days," Vietti said dreamily.

She was huddled on the sofa. He put his hand on Odile's neck and pulled her face down to his waist. After that, the worst part of it for her was feeling the pressure of his manicured fingers in her hair.

The lights at the Café des Sports were off. She took a right down boulevard Gouvion-Saint-Cyr. The roll of bills Viette had given her was buried in one of the pockets of her raincoat: two thousand francs. He had said, looking snide, that she "cost a lot for a whore," but that it wasn't any problem for him, because he had "always liked expensive whores" for as long as he could remember.

She crossed avenue des Ternes and looked down toward where Bellune had killed himself. Suddenly she felt his absence with such force that it was as though she had plunged into the void. What would Bellune have thought about all this? He hadn't believed very strongly in her future as a singer either, and near the end he was obviously preoccupied with other things. But she remembered her afternoon visits to his office, and the deck of his apartment where you felt like you were on the bridge of an ocean liner. It was Bellune who had taught her "La Chanson des rues," a song dating from the time when he had first come to France. He had always shown kindness to her. His face, bent over the tape player while the reel turned in silence. And the words he used to say, in a soft voice, before leading her out of his office:

"What do you say we go downstairs, Odile?"

And Louis? What would he think if he knew what had just happened? He would never know. She needed the money. Bejardy's fifteen hundred francs was not enough, and the only way the two of them could escape was by having money.

She had earned more money that night than Louis's monthly salary, and she was sorry she hadn't demanded more from that bastard with the manicured fingernails. She heard again the nightclub manager's laugh, after he told her she wouldn't be singing there anymore. She should have gotten some money out of him too.

The dream was over. She would not sing again. She had not succeeded in making people hear; her voice had not freed itself from the dust and the noise like the voice of the singer she had read about. She did not have the courage.

She reached rue Delaizement, with the garage at the end. The light on the second floor was on and Louis was asleep on the couch. The large album where he glued photographs of his father was sitting on the floor, next to an open volume of the bound issues of the sports magazine. He had glued an article at the top of the album page and she read it mechanically:

"... In the following stage, Memling finally had the upper hand over Gérardin, who started too cautiously, and overtook him at the 3,625 meter mark..."

She turned out the light and curled up against Louis.

LATER, when the two of them talked about the past—but they did so only on very rare occasions, mostly after the birth of their children—they were surprised to realize that the most decisive time in their lives had lasted barely seven months. It was true: Louis had left the army in December, they had met in early January...

In February, Brossier found them a new apartment. One day, when he came to see Louis at Porte Champerret, he was shocked by how tiny the room was and the stifling heat from the enormous radiator.

"You can't stay here, old boy. Why didn't you ever tell me about this?"

He knew about a "two bedroom" available just then, which he'd wanted to rent himself but then he had changed his mind, it was too far away from Cité Universitaire. It was at the start of rue Caulaincourt, on the other side of the iron bridge that crossed over Montmartre Cemetery. The rent? Reasonable, very reasonable. He would talk to Bejardy about it. Bejardy wouldn't have the heart to leave Odile and Louis in such a miniscule, overheated attic.

They moved into the place on rue Caulaincourt the following month, and the apartment felt enormous. The main room was a studio. In one corner—the only things left from the artist who had lived there—there were a fan with huge blades and a semicircular bar. The bar's chipped black lacquer was decorated with Chinese-inspired drawings like the ones on the shirt Brossier liked to wear at Cité. The windows looked out over southwest Paris.

Bejardy gave them a bed and an armchair with garnet-red upholstery, Brossier two cane chairs and a lamp. They even had a phone. And a well-furnished kitchen. When the concierge asked for their names to put on his list of renters, they said Mr. and Mrs. Memling, thinking he would feel better about a young married couple.

One night, they had their official housewarming party, as Brossier pompously put it. He said that Jacqueline Boivin, his fiancée, would unfortunately not be able to join them—from Cité Universitaire, rue Caulaincourt seemed like the other end of the world. You had to cross the Seine to get there, and the river was the frontier between two cities that had nothing to do with each other.

Bejardy came. Louis noticed a green and yellow ribbon on the lapel of his jacket.

"You've been decorated?" he asked.

"The Médaille militaire," Bejardy said. "I earned it in Germany, under Marshal de Lattre. I was twenty-three. It's the only good thing I've ever done in my life."

He lowered his eyes, and it was clear he wanted to change the subject.

They had aperitifs in the studio. Then they had dinner nearby, at Chez Justin on rue Joseph de Maistre.

He no longer worked nights. From that point on, Bejardy entrusted him with "little tasks" to be carried out during the day, or else he would stay in the garage to greet visitors and answer the phone. These "little tasks" consisted in bringing letters to or from various addresses in Paris and the surrounding areas; Bejardy had told him he didn't trust the mail. Often he would act as a chauffeur, driving Bejardy to his meetings in an old English car with a leather smell. His salary had been doubled, without Bejardy saying anything to explain why.

He felt vaguely uneasy. What was his "job" exactly? What "company" was he working for? And Bejardy? Why had he made him his right-hand man so quickly?

He rarely shared these doubts with Odile. On the contrary, his years of solitude, at boarding school and in the army, had given him the habit of not trusting anyone, concealing his worries. He forced himself to seem calm around her, and convinced her that his job was respectable. Bejardy's protective attitude could be explained by the fact that he used to know his father. This was only a half lie: Bejardy had told him that he had been a cycling enthusiast in his youth and that he was delighted to be in a position to give Memling the cyclist's son a job.

No, he couldn't show the least unease around Odile. To do so would mean risking the fragile equilibrium of their life together. They no longer lived in a garret, after all, but in an apartment on rue Caulaincourt. And you could read, right there in black and white, on the list of renters stuck on the concierge's window: "Mr. and Mrs. Memling." Not bad for a twenty year old.

But he did let himself ask Brossier some questions. They were sitting in one of the booths at the Rêve, a café on rue Caulaincourt that Louis liked for its name: Café Dream. It amused him and Odile to say, "See you at the Dream at five."

"You don't trust Roland, do you?"

"No, it's not that . . ."

"Roland is a good guy, old boy. Not everyone gets the Médaille militaire at twenty-three."

"I know."

"You're doing very ordinary work. It's boring. I don't mean that as an insult. It's a job like a messenger's, or a bellhop's. There's nothing suspicious about that, is there?"

He gave him a friendly clap on the shoulder.

"I'm joking. You're more like Roland's secretary. Me too, for that matter. You think that's anything to be ashamed of?"

"No, but what exactly does Roland do?"

"Roland is a businessman, with an interest in cars, and other things," Brossier answered carefully, as though reciting a lesson.

"How did you meet him?"

"I'll tell you someday when we have more time."

They had left and were walking down the street. A crowd of children bursting out of the school yard jostled them. One of them was wearing roller skates and the others were chasing him.

"You're nervous, I understand," Brossier said in his husky voice, a little breathless, the voice he used to talk about matters close to his heart.

This was not the blustering Brossier anymore. How strange, Louis thought—that a person can have two different voices like that.

He was saying that at Louis's age, one often has rather vague and boring tasks to perform; you have to make do however you can. Things get clearer later, but when you're twenty they're still in a rough and sketchy state. Everything is hazy. That's life in the beginning, old boy. I myself… One day, I'll tell you everything.

She tried to keep busy while Louis was out. She had kept a friend named Mary from her time at the cabaret-restaurant in Auteuil; Mary still worked there. She sang and danced for a few minutes, accompanied by a group of balalaika players and dressed in a "Ukrainian princess" costume, which looked more like an outfit from the Tyrolean Alps. But the folklore act was nothing more than a temporary way to earn some money. Her dream was to open a little fashion boutique. She discussed it with Odile and they made plans to go into business together.

In the meantime, Mary could work at home and build up a clientele. Odile wondered how they could pull together enough money to open the shop. They had already decided on its name, Chez Mary Bakradzé, thinking the strange name would work in their favor. Under "Chez Mary Bakradzé," in capital letters, it would say "MODE— FASHION," a label Odile had admired on the pediment of a store in the Saint-Honoré neighborhood.

Mary drew the patterns and knew how to cut the fabric. She had worked for a dressmaker, a friend of the family, when she was very young. Odile asked her about her parents but never got a straight answer: Sometimes Mary said her father and mother were separated and living abroad; sometimes they were living in a house in the south of France and would be coming to visit her any day now; sometimes they had disappeared. The one fixed point in the fog—the only member of the family who had left any visible trace—was Mary's grandfather, a writer exiled to Paris, one Paul Bakradzé. He devoted his talents to portraying, in delicate brushstrokes, life in a military garrison in southern Russia. One of his novels had even been translated into French, and Mary piously kept a worn old copy of it.

She was blond, petite, with very fair, almost pink skin and pale blue eyes.

Odile and Louis saw her on Sundays. Mary lived in the area between avenue de la Grande-Armée and avenue Foch, a hybrid zone where the sixteenth arrondissement becomes solid and residential but the streets are still under the sway of the garages, stores selling bicycles or ball bearings, old dance halls, and the ghost of the old Luna Park.

The three of them would stroll in the Bois de Boulogne, from Porte Dauphine to the lakes. There, they would take a rowboat and paddle for an hour. Or else they would moor at the dock of the Chalet des Îles and play a game of miniature golf. When it got dark, they would go back to Mary's apartment: three rooms, with the first two serving as anteroom and living room. The third, at the end of a long hall, was Mary's bedroom.

When they arrived, ten or so people would be crowded into the living room. Older people, some of them quite elderly, playing bridge or chatting over tea. Mary hugged a woman of about sixty as she walked past—tall, moon-faced, with slanting eyes and the authority of mistress of the house. Her aunt, Mary told Louis and Odile.

The gathering talked or played cards in the dimly lit room. Every time, Mary would light the lamps and the chandelier, as though this task had been left to her because the others thought it was too hard to flip a switch, or beneath their dignity. Or maybe the idea never crossed their minds.

In Mary's room, they listened to records and talked. Odile and Louis had found in her the carefree laziness that was actually natural to them both. They were all the same age, born the same year. They understood one another, and Odile and Louis often stayed the night.

Mary would bring them something to eat, a piece of cake or a bowl of soup. They would hear the murmur of voices in the living room through the half-open door. Little by little, the conversations would die out, the people would leave. A man would be talking on the phone in the hall. He would be quiet for long stretches, and they would think he had hung up every time, but then he would say something else, before falling silent again. This conventicle in an unknown language on the phone would go on for hours, often until morning.

One Sunday, one of Mary's friends came by, a young Spaniard their age named Jordan. He was looking for cabaret work with his drag-queen number. On Mary's suggestion, he had introduced himself to the manager of the Auteuil nightclub and been hired for a trial period.

He would be starting there in a few days, and he wanted a stage dress like the one the heroine wore in an illustrated edition of Louÿs's *The Woman and the Puppet* that he had found at one of the used-book stalls on the quais. Mary and Odile decided to make him one, and spent days cutting and stitching in Mary's room while Louis read a mystery novel. At each fitting, Jordan asked Louis for his opinion. The dress looked good on him, and with his soft features, under his mantilla, the illusion was very convincing.

The evening of his debut, Louis and Odile went to the nightclub. Jordan was on after Mary. The balalaikas fell silent and, in the darkness, a deep voice announced: "La Cigarrera!"

The first notes of Hummel's *Bolero* sounded, which Jordan was going to dance to; he had brought the tape himself. When the lights came on, Jordan was standing in the middle of the stage, pale and paralyzed in his dress.

The castanets fell from his hand like dead fruit. He stood there unmoving for several seconds, then collapsed on the floor. He had fainted from stage fright—or hunger, since he had eaten almost nothing for two weeks, afraid of losing his "figure" and not being able to fit into his dress for the act.

He was fired on the spot, and Odile, Louis, and Mary had to console him.

ON THE first day of spring, Bejardy invited Odile and Louis out to lunch, and the two of them decided to take advantage of the sun by walking the whole way to Quai Louis-Blériot.

Brossier opened the door and brought them into the living room, where a table had been set for five. Bejardy was with a young brunette, the one whose photograph Louis had noticed on the mantelpiece the first day.

"Nicole Haas, a friend . . . Mr. and Mrs. Memling . . . You remember, Coco, it's Mrs. Memling, who sings 'La Chanson des rues' so beautifully."

He always called them that, in a ceremonious tone, because he'd thought it was funny when he read "Mr. and Mrs. Memling" on the list of tenants in their apartment building.

"Good idea," he'd told Louis. "That looks more serious. Now you need to get married. I'll be your best man if you want."

Nicole Haas had an elegant face but severe features. She was tall, almost Bejardy's height, and Louis was struck by her boyish looks, especially her way of smoking and of sitting with her legs outstretched, high heels resting on the low table.

"Dinner is served, monsieur," Brossier said formally.

"Louis, sit on Coco's right. Mrs. Memling on my right..."

No one spoke much during lunch. Nicole Haas, at the head of the table, seemed to be in a bad mood. Bejardy gazed lovingly at her. She was younger than him—barely thirty.

"Are you going riding this afternoon, Coco?" Bejardy asked.

"No. I have to go to Equistable. I need a saddle."

She pouted and, with a nonchalant gesture, poured herself a large glass of water.

"Equistable is a good place to buy one, I think," Brossier said.

She shrugged. "Yes, but I usually go to Ramaget."

She seemed annoyed at Bejardy and Brossier, but curious about and friendly toward Odile and Louis.

"Do you ride?"

"No," Odile said.

"Why haven't you ever invited them to Vertbois?" she asked Bejardy.

"We'll invite them this summer, Nicole."

She turned back to Odile and Louis and smiled at them.

"If he brings you to Vertbois, I'll teach you how to ride a horse."

"Vertbois is a...family property, in Sologne," Bejardy said. "You'll have to see it sometime."

"Vertbois is the cradle of the Counts of Bejardy," Nicole Haas said ironically. "Second Empire 'nobility.' Roland added the 'de' himself."

This time, Bejardy lost his temper, and the subservient look he had been giving Nicole Haas grew hard.

"Nonsense, Coco. Louis, my boy, you have before you a textbook case of snobbery. Nicole here is obsessed with the aristocracy."

Nicole Haas burst out laughing and lit a cigarette.

"Stop, you fool." Loving contempt for Bejardy shone through her words.

A tray with coffee was waiting on the desk on the other side of the room. In the hall, Nicole Haas opened a window and the wind billowed the gauze curtains. Bejardy served the coffee himself.

Nicole Haas, Odile, and Louis were sitting on the velvet sofa. Bejardy and Brossier, leaning on the desk, kept silent, perhaps afraid to provoke a bad-tempered word from Nicole Haas. But she was ignoring them.

She took a leather cigarette case out of her bag and held it out to Odile, then to Louis. She lit their cigarettes herself, with a lighter that had a high flame. Louis was surprised to see it in her hand: It was one of the Zippo lighters from the American army that they had tried to get ahold of at all costs when he was in boarding school.

"Coco, do you want me to come with you to Equistable?"

But she turned to Louis: "You have a nice name, Monsieur de Memling."

"His name is just Memling, no 'de,' " Bejardy said.

She didn't listen to him. She smoked her cigarette and watched the gauze curtains, bathed in sunlight, that the wind was waving back and forth like a fluttering scarf.

Nicole Haas suddenly stood up and went over to the ashtray on Bejardy's desk to put out her cigarette.

"I have to go."

"Do you need the car?" Bejardy asked.

"No."

She shook hands with Odile and Louis.

"I hope to see you again."

And, without paying the least attention to Bejardy, she headed for the door.

"See you tonight, Coco," Bejardy said. "Be good."

She did not even take the trouble to turn around, and shut the door behind her. Brossier gave a little nervous smile. Bejardy sat down on the sofa, next to Odile and Louis, and sighed.

"She's not a bad girl, despite how it looks. Louis, I have to talk to you . . . Let's go to the next room for a minute."

"Tell me, Madame Memling, would you care to play a game of chess while they're talking?" Brossier suggested.

"Why not?" Odile said, keeping her eye on Louis as Bejardy led him into the next room with a hand on his shoulder, a gesture meant to be protective and friendly.

They walked into the room where Odile and Louis had spent the night. The bright Citroën factory building on the other side of the Seine looked like it belonged in an airfield.

"Nice view, hmm?" Bejardy said. "When I started out, I had a garage in that neighborhood there, across the river. Rue Balard. Back when I would go see your father race . . . I saw him race for the first time in 1938, at the Vel' d'Hiv. I was sixteen."

"Did you know him?" Louis asked.

"No. I knew Aerts, and Charles Pélissier, but I spent more time with automobile people."

Was it the mention of his father, or the term Bejardy used, "automobile people," which sounded a bit like "captains of industry" or "gentleman rider"? Whatever the reason, Louis suddenly saw himself in a large, chilly, unused garage. Rays of sunlight were falling through a glass roof. The branches outside traced shadows on the floor like the shadows of leaves on the surface of a lake.

His childhood.

Bejardy had lain down on the bed and was resting his feet on the padded bedposts so as not to get the satin bedspread dirty. Louis stayed standing, by the window.

"So here it is. I need you to do something for me. You're taking a little trip to England."

In the living room, sitting at the low table, Brossier and Odile were absorbed in their chess game. Odile had acquired a taste for it under Mary's influence; it was Mary who had taught her and Louis how the pieces moved.

Bejardy and Louis followed the game in silence. After ten or fifteen minutes, Odile said checkmate. Brossier was not a very expert player either.

"A formidable opponent, our little Mrs. Memling," Brossier said with a smile.

Outside, they walked in the direction of Porte d'Auteuil. The streets were deserted. Now and then a bus would pass, and its whir would dissipate in the sunlight.

They felt light, as if they were breathing in the open air again after a long time underwater. Maybe, Louis thought, it was because winter was over. He remembered back to December, leaving his barracks with his soggy shoes. The swishy watery noise they made with every step gave him the feeling of being permanently bogged down. Now he would happily run barefoot on the dry sidewalk.

"What are you thinking about?" Odile asked him, taking his arm.

"We're going to England. I'll explain . . ."

"To England?"

She was unfazed. This afternoon, anything seemed possible to her.

They eventually reached the edge of the Bois de Boulogne. Loud groups of people were making their way to the racetrack entrance.

"Let's take a boat ride," Louis said.

On their way to the lake, they changed their mind. The wind gently stirring the leaves and scattering the children's laughs and screams, the sun, the prospect of this trip to England—it all made them lazy. They sat down at an outdoor table at the Auteuil farm and ordered two cherry milks.

They didn't talk. Odile rested her head on Louis's shoulder and drank her white grenadine through a straw. Down on the riding path, an Amazonian brunette riding a spotted gray horse passed slowly by, and they thought they recognized Nicole Haas.

Just after the Russian Orthodox Easter, which they celebrated with Mary, Brossier set up an appointment for them at the "French-English Youth Exchange" office across the street from the Opéra Comique. He was signing them up to spend their holidays in Bournemouth, the seaside resort in Hampshire.

In a narrow room cluttered with folders, they were received by a Mr. "A. Stewart," according to the name they saw on a brass plate on the door. He was in his eighties, with wrinkles around his eyes and mottled skin. All their papers were ready. Louis and Odile only had to give their dates of birth.

"I said that you're students," Stewart said in the voice of an insect. "It's better that way."

"You're right," Brossier said.

"Of course you're not obligated to stay to the end," Stewart said.

"I know," Louis said.

"How's Roland?" Stewart asked.

"He's fine."

He walked them to the door.

"I knew Roland de Bejardy's father very well," Stewart said, suddenly serious, turning to Odile and Louis. "We were close friends."

Brossier had things to do and asked Louis to take Bejardy's car, which the three of them had used to go to the Youth Exchange office on rue Favart. Odile and Louis walked at random and sat down at an outdoor café table on rue Réaumur, near the window. There was a copy of the financial newspaper, *Cote Desfossés*, on the table.

Louis, for appearances' sake, flipped through the paper and his eyes were drawn to the Unlisted Securities section. The time had come to tell Odile the reason for this trip to England, but he didn't know how to bring up the delicate subject.

"Is that interesting?"

She held out her hand with a smile for the *Cote Desfossés*, and put it aside on the bench next to her. Louis looked at her, uncertainly.

"What are you thinking about?"

"Nothing. The stock market. Look."

He pointed to the Bourse on the other side of the street, with its colonnade and the stairs with the groups of businessmen walking down them. It was raining. More and more customers came into the café and gathered at the counter. Most of them were carrying black briefcases. At the table next to theirs, a man, still quite young but red in the face, with sparse black hair combed back, looked up occasionally from the folder he was studying and rudely stared at Odile.

"So, this trip to England. It's to do something for Bejardy."

Taking a deep breath, he gave her the details in a rush, as though afraid she might interrupt him. All the details. That he was supposed to bring almost five hundred thousand francs in cash into England for Bejardy, that he would get a percentage of it, and that the trick was to join a French-English Youth Exchange group to avoid customs. Stewart, the director of the youth exchange, was in on the scheme, it seemed.

She listened with her eyes wide, and when he was finished they were silent for a moment.

"They must have been planning this from the start. I'm sure of it," she said.

"Yes, definitely..."

Louis shrugged. They'd just have to see what happened. He knew she was thinking the same thing.

"Well, it's nothing too bad, all this."

They were living through one of those moments when you feel the need to grab on to something stable and solid, the longing to ask someone for advice. But there wasn't anyone. Except for the gray silhouettes with their black briefcases crossing rue Réaumur in the rain, coming into the café, having their coffee or drink at the counter, and leaving. Their movements made Odile and Louis feel numb. The ground was shifting under their feet.

They walked through the concourse at Gare Saint-Lazare, and Brossier wanted to stop at the little café in the passageway between the station and the Hotel Terminus.

"No, I think it'd be better for us downstairs," Louis said. "Near the departure platform."

Odile looked at him and smiled.

"This place has bad memories for us," he said.

So they headed for the cafeteria at the back and sat down. The meeting place was at the entrance to the passageway leading to the departure platforms. A group of young people was standing a few feet away. Louis looked at his watch: It was almost the meeting time.

"That's the youth exchange group, isn't it?" Louis asked Brossier.

"It must be."

Brossier tried and failed to suppress a laugh, and Odile caught it.

"You think it's funny?" Louis asked. But in the end he laughed too.

"I hope you study hard," Brossier said. "Learn a lot of English, with the others."

Louis had put a large canvas backpack, with lots of pockets, on a chair next to him. It contained some of the bundles of banknotes, hidden in shirts and sweaters. The rest of the money was concealed at the bottom of Odile's cardboard valise.

"Time to join the others now," Brossier said.

He helped Louis put on his blue backpack, like a camper's or mountaineer's. Odile carried her little cardboard suitcase herself.

They went over to the edge of the group, with Brossier.

"You'll call us when you get there, right?" Brossier said.

"You really think there won't be any problems?" Louis said.

"None. I'll leave you now. Give me a kiss."

The suggestion surprised him, coming from Brossier, who exchanged kisses on the cheek with Odile too. Then he left. He turned around at the top of the stairs and waved, before he disappeared.

"You're with us?" a young man with very large lips and a crew cut asked Odile.

"Yes."

"Great. Over here . . ."

They shook hands with about ten young people who introduced themselves by first name. The crew-cut guy seemed to be in charge of the group.

"Here, stick these on your luggage and the back of your jackets."

He showed Odile and Louis little triangular labels saying YOUTH EXCHANGE, and attached them himself to their coats, backpack, and suitcase.

"If they come off, I'll give you more."

Most of their traveling companions already knew each other. They brought up a previous stay in Bournemouth and talked about someone named Axter, whose name Louis had heard from Bejardy.

"Who's Axter?" Louis asked the guy he thought of as the group leader from then on.

"Mr. Axter is the head of the school where we'll be taking courses."

"Courses?"

"Yes, every morning."

"Is this the first time you two are going to England with the youth exchange?" a brunette with blue eyes asked.

"Yes," Louis said.

"It's really great, you'll see."

"Well, I think it's time," the crew-cut guy with the big lips said.

The train to Le Havre was waiting on the platform. The crew-cut guy handed a group ticket to the ticket controller.

"How many?"

"Twelve."

The controller distractedly counted them as they proceeded onto the platform.

"Can I go buy some magazines?" Odile asked.

"Hurry," the crew-cut guy said. "And if you see *Science and Life*, buy me one?"

"I'll go with you," Louis said.

They walked quickly. As they left the platform, they showed the ticket controller their Youth Exchange stickers.

At the kiosk, Louis bought *Elle*, *Candide*, *Match*, *Paris-Presse*, and *Science and Life*. Odile waited, sitting on her suitcase, absentmindedly watching the people come and go, more and more of them since rush hour was approaching. Suddenly her heart was pounding and she was almost suffocating: She had seen the fat blond, the policeman who had used her as bait. He walked by not far from her and slowly headed for the entrance to the café.

The youth exchange group had reserved two compartments, and Odile and Louis sat face-to-face next to the door. She had put her suitcase up on the luggage rack and Louis kept his blue backpack in his hands. She was thinking about the fat blond and felt demoralized, caught in a trap. That deposition she had signed ... They had kept it in a file somewhere. So what. But maybe the fat blond had found evidence to link her to Bellune's apartment? She thought she might have left one of her flexi-discs there, and some photographs of her that Bellune had wanted for a record cover ... But what if he wasn't on that case? Well, she had seen him at avenue des Ternes, in front of the Hotel Rovaro.

Louis was talking to the others. Little by little, she started listening to them, and eventually forgot about the fat blond.

She was sitting next to a girl who admitted to her that she was only seventeen. She looked older because of her height, her sunglasses, and her deep voice. The brunette with blue eyes and a pleated skirt was sitting to Louis's right. There was another girl with a chubby face, and a brown-haired boy who clearly thought he was very handsome. He wore a signet ring and never stopped running his hand through his hair.

"What about you?" he asked Odile and Louis. "You have your families' addresses?"

They didn't understand what he meant. Our families? Yes, the members of the youth exchange lived with families during their stay in Bournemouth. But Odile and Louis did not know their families' addresses.

At Le Havre, they waited for departure at a café table on the pier. The jukebox was playing Italian songs, and the melodious sound of their words got swallowed up by the mist and concrete all around.

The boat was at the dock. The crew-cut guy told Odile and Louis that it was called the *Normania* and that it would travel to Southampton overnight.

The customs office was in a kind of small hangar. The crew-cut guy had collected all the passports from the group members; when Odile handed hers over, she had a fleeting memory of the fat blond policeman.

One of the customs officers stamped the passports one after the other and gave them back to the youth exchange group leader, who seemed to know him.

"Lots of passengers tonight?"

"Not bad," the customs officer answered. "It's Easter break. Look."

Groups of teenagers, boys and girls between fifteen and twenty, were standing packed together on the *Normania*'s deck. Some were singing a song. When the youth exchange members boarded, they could hardly make their way through the crush of people. The crew-cut guy waved with one hand and held Louis's wrist tightly with the other.

"Don't lose sight of us. We'll meet up in the grand salon. Make sure you keep your badges on you...Yes...Yes... Keep them on you, that's the most important thing. I gave them to you, keep them on."

The poor man, he was horrified at the thought that the youth exchange group might get split up in the crowd. His voice, which up until then had suggested a sheepdog's bark, was almost a sob.

Night had long since fallen by the time the *Normania* cast off. Odile and Louis, leaning on the ship's railing, looked out at the lights of Le Havre getting farther and farther away. Louis was still wearing his blue backpack and Odile clutched her suitcase between her legs. Nearby, ten or fifteen young people in large black velvet berets were singing an old ballad in the gentle breeze, in a language they didn't recognize. The group alternated in halves, repeating the chorus, and Odile and Louis relaxed and let the melodious unknown language wash over them.

Before long, the deck was empty except for them. Neither one felt the cold air—this was their first time traveling by ship. They walked to the stern and then down a staircase and along gangways where small groups of people, sitting on the ground, were chatting and playing cards. A bit farther up, people were crowding around a metal counter to buy a sandwich or a warm drink. Eventually they came out into what the group leader had called the "salon," but which looked more like a smoking lounge, with leather sofas and armchairs bolted to the floor and landscape photos on the paneled walls like the pictures in train compartments. There were two portholes, one on each side, and a bridge table in front of one of them.

As soon as they walked in, the smell of pipes and brown tobacco seized them by the throat. Here, as well, passengers were sitting around on the floor. Some were even asleep in their sleeping bags. The youth exchange group was gathered around a sofa and an armchair, and the crew-cut group leader waved Louis and Odile over. Louis carried Odile's suitcase on his shoulder and the two of them forced their way through the outstretched bodies and the groups sitting cross-legged. Near the bridge table, three of the mysterious beret-clad strangers were still singing, in a subdued voice.

"I thought you were lost," the group leader said. "Sit over here. Why are you still carrying your luggage? That doesn't make sense, you should have left it with ours."

Louis shrugged his shoulders in response. He sat down on the floor, his back against the side of the sofa, and Odile found a place next to him.

"We use first names in our group," the leader said. "My name's Gilbert."

He introduced the blue-eyed brunette with the pleated skirt and the boy with the signet ring: "Françoise, Alain." Then the others.

"Marie-Jo, Claude, Christian…"

Louis and Odile said their names in turn.

"You're brother and sister?" Gilbert asked.

"No, cousins," Louis said without thinking.

The ship had started to rock and now the movement grew more noticeable.

"I hope you don't get seasick," Gilbert said. "It usually doesn't last long. The crossing is pretty smooth, actually."

He took a pipe out of his pocket.

"Personally, I have a radical cure for seasickness: a pipe! Axter and me, we agree about that. He's a great one for pipe-smoking too."

Odile curled up, closed her eyes, and rested her cheek against the back of the sofa. Gilbert lit his pipe. With his crew cut and large lips, he looked like a good little schoolboy, and Louis imagined him in short pants, at the top of the class, raising a finger every time the teacher asked a question and saying, "M'sieu! M'sieu!"

On the armchair, the dark-haired boy with the ring was flirting with Marie-Jo, the girl who seemed older than her seventeen years. Then he kissed her, interminably. His arms were crossed behind the girl's neck and Louis suspected him of glancing secretly at his wristwatch to time how long the kiss lasted.

"You don't want a puff, do you, old boy?" Gilbert said.

He offered him the pipe. Louis refused.

"Your cousin is asleep, old boy," Gilbert said, pointing to Odile.

The ship rocked more and more. Odile's suitcase, sitting at the foot of the sofa, slid a little and Louis caught it. He had put his backpack back on.

"Wearing that pack doesn't bother you, old boy?" Gilbert said.

"No," Louis said. "I'm used to it."

The dark-haired boy and Marie-Jo were still in their embrace. Other romances were springing up between members of the group. The chubby-cheeked girl was holding hands with a short redheaded boy whose accent sounded French Algerian. The brunette with the blue eyes and pleated skirt seemed jealous of Marie-Jo, held close by the dark-haired boy.

"The problem is that they won't learn English because they'll spend all their time pairing up with each other," Gilbert said. "I'll have to have a talk with Axter about it. Good-for-nothings . . . Now you and your cousin are setting a good example, at least. That's how it should be."

One of the mysterious singers by the bridge table was feeling seasick and holding his large velvet beret ready in case he needed to throw up in it.

"We'll get to Southampton around seven in the morning," Gilbert said, with his pipe between his teeth.

Odile opened her eyes and looked sleepily at Louis. Just then, the lights flickered and went out. There were shouts and exclamations from all sides. Someone, who sounded like he was from the south of France, shouted: "Fuck the Queen of England!"

Laughter. A hubbub of conversation. Hiccups, no doubt from one of the singers with the velvet berets, Louis thought. Several voices shouting in unison: "Lights! Liii-ights!"

Some people lit their cigarette lighters. Louis leaned over to Odile.

"Let's go to bed," he whispered in her ear.

He picked up Odile's suitcase and they left the "salon," trying their best to avoid the tangle of bodies on the floor. A dim light was coming from the gangway.

Eventually they found the corridor of cabins, and Louis took a ticket out of his pocket to check for their number. Two couchettes. They lay down. Louis clutched the backpack and suitcase tight and wondered what their group leader would think if he knew that Odile and he had a cabin, which Brossier had reserved for them back in Paris. Gilbert would surely be hurt that these two cousins were not sleeping in the salon with the rest of the "youth exchange."

Everything was floating in a white mist. Disembarking from the *Normania*, they passed through English customs and Gilbert took them to a bus waiting on the pier.

A man in the back of the bus greeted Gilbert.

"How are you, Mr. Axter?"

"Well, thank you. And you? Was it a pleasant crossing?"

He spoke French with a very slight accent. A blond man, in his forties, with curly hair and big tortoiseshell glasses, a red tweed vest, and a pipe.

The members of the group sat down in the bus, with Odile and Louis sitting a little farther back. Axter looked worriedly around the group.

"Tell me, Gilbert, do you have in your group a certain . . . Louis Memling?"

"Louis? Louis? Ah, yes, the cousins."

He pointed out Louis and Odile.

Axter smiled at them.

"Michel Axter," he said. "Pleased to make your acquaintance."

There was a certain coquetterie in the way he Frenchified his first name. He shook hands with Louis and Odile and then sat down across the aisle from them, keeping his head turned to face them.

"Roland de Bejardy phoned me last night to let me know you were coming. He is a very good friend of mine, you know."

He stuffed his pipe, a smile fixed to his face. Gilbert kept a respectful distance, surprised at this sudden intimacy between Axter and Louis and Odile. Surprised and maybe a bit jealous, too.

"I would go so far as to say that Roland and I are childhood friends."

This time his face opened up in a real smile. Gilbert, more and more taken aback, nervously brought out his pipe, as though trying to win back Axter's attention with the gesture and reestablish the complicity between them. He stammered: "Still a fan of the Amsterdammer, sir?"

But Axter wasn't listening. He leaned toward Odile and Louis.

"I am so pleased to welcome you to our school in Bournemouth."

Then, from where he was sitting, he counted the members of group with his index finger.

"Everyone here?"

"Everyone is here, Mr. Axter," Gilbert said.

"All right, tell the driver."

The bus started and Gilbert sat back down, very near Axter, Odile, and Louis. He was probably afraid that they would say bad things about him if he wasn't there.

"It won't be long. Bournemouth is very close by," Axter said.

"So how is your wife?" Gilbert asked, desperately trying to get Axter's attention.

But Axter opened a newspaper and read it with great composure.

Outside the windows, everything disappeared in a bright white fog, and Louis wondered by what miracle the driver was able to see where he was going.

A few minutes before they reached Bournemouth, the sun reappeared, which prompted Axter to say, "You see, it's always sunny in Bournemouth."

Gilbert, not wanting to pass up a chance to rejoin the conversation, added: "It's a Mediterranean climate. Lots of pine trees, and flowers. As Mr. Axter has often remarked, Bournemouth is the Cannes of Dorset."

His fawning fell flat. Axter shrugged his shoulders.

He took a list out of his pocket and, turning to face Odile and Louis, said, "We'll drop off the young people with the families they're staying with. It won't take long."

"We're arriving at Christchurch, sir," Gilbert said gravely, sounding like the guide on a jungle expedition, pointing out a path to his client.

Axter checked his list.

"We have someone getting out at Christchurch. Marie-José Quinili, with the Guilfords. 23 Meryl Lane. Tell the driver to stop at 23 Meryl Lane."

Gilbert obeyed.

And the same ceremony took place every time. The bus stopped at the address on the list, a cottage or little house with a garden in front. The family was waiting outside: mother and children on the stoop, father on the sidewalk in front of the open garden gate, all standing at attention, so to speak. Axter stepped out of the bus with the boy or girl from the group, whom he introduced to the father. Gilbert followed behind them, carrying the student's suitcase. Then the father, Axter, and the youth exchange student walked over to the stoop, where a short conversation took place with the members of the family, while Gilbert put the suitcase down. Then the father walked Axter and Gilbert back to the bus. The exchange student stayed on the stoop with the mother and children, and they all stiffly watched the bus, again, as it left.

There was no one left in the bus except Axter, Gilbert, Odile, and Louis. Gilbert was getting more and more anxious.

"I'll take you to Cross Road, the same family as last year," Axter said.

"Thank you. That way I'm very near you . . ." He paused. Then he blurted out: "And them? What family are they staying with?"

"They're staying with me, at the school."

Gilbert stared wide-eyed. "With you?"

He looked like he had just been punched in the stomach. He face crumpled and his lips were bigger than ever, as though pumped full of air, pneumatically somehow, and about to burst.

"Why with you?"

"Just because. Does that surprise you?"

The bus stopped at Cross Road, in front of a tidy little cottage with a white picket fence around the garden.

"Here you are, Gilbert."

Gilbert didn't move, trying to delay the moment of parting. Axter picked up his suitcase. Gilbert had no choice but to stand up sadly.

"They're lucky they get to stay with you," he said in a wheezing voice.

Axter put Gilbert's suitcase down at the garden gate and shook his hand, then rejoined Odile and Louis in the bus.

Gilbert stayed unmoving, in front of the cottage, ignoring his suitcase. His face was alarmingly pale and he eyed Odile and Louis hungrily, lips curled, until the moment the bus started. Louis was amazed at the envy and hate in Gilbert's eyes.

"He's not a bad kid, but he is a bit clingy," Axter said.

A sandy lane snaking past a closely mowed lawn and masses of rhododendrons led to the house, a big Norman-style mansion with a bell tower soaring overhead. A white marble plaque above the entrance bore the inscription: BOSCOMBE COLLEGE.

"Here we are," Axter said. "Let me show you to your room."

They walked down a hallway with classrooms visible through the open doors.

"The classes are held here," Axter said. "Every morning. Of course, it's not required that you attend."

He winked at Odile and Louis, which came as a surprise from this Englishman.

They walked upstairs to the fourth floor. Axter opened a door. They went down another hallway that ended in an attic room with white walls and not a single piece of furniture. There was a mattress on the floor, covered in pink sheets and a Scottish wool blanket.

"Here you have the bathroom," Axter said.

A frosted glass booth with a sink and shower.

"I think you'll be fine here. I've just renovated this floor of the building."

He took Odile's suitcase and Louis's backpack, opened the room's closet, and began putting their clothes on the shelves. Louis wanted to stop him.

"No, *please...*"

Odile and Louis exchanged a shocked look. Axter arranged their shirts, sweaters, dresses, and pants, in impeccable order.

"This is fun. It reminds me of when I was back at Trinity College."

When everything was in its place, he took the bundles of banknotes out of the backpack and suitcase with the most natural-looking gesture imaginable.

He slipped them one by one into a large green plastic bag he had taken out of his pocket and unfolded like a handkerchief. Then he turned to Odile and Louis.

"Now you can call Roland de Bejardy and tell him that everything went well."

The telephone was in the hall, attached to the wall. Axter spoke in English. He nodded his head to the instructions that Bejardy must have been giving him.

"Cheerio, Roland. Give my regards to Nicole."

Then he passed the phone to Louis.

"Study hard and learn English well," Bejardy told him. "It will serve you well in life."

They were woken up around nine in the morning by the voices of the students walking across the lawn. There were more than fifty young men and women attending Boscombe

College and Louis saw Gilbert among them, with his pipe and his clenched jaw. He went from group to group, wearing a Scottish kilt and a turtleneck sweater.

Odile and Louis had wanted to take the classes but they would have had to get up early, and besides, the students taking English at Boscombe College, although close to them in age, seemed like strangers. What could they talk about? Nothing. They did not share the same worries. The bell rang three times to indicate a break, and the young people scattered across the grass. Pairs were always kissing, assiduously, as though timing their sessions. A happy, unspoiled adolescence, perfectly sure of itself. Axter charged a lot of money for the classes at Boscombe and recruited customers from the families of the seventh or sixteenth arrondissements, or in a pinch from among the rich French Algerians.

The two of them stayed in bed, pressed against each other, and listened to the serious voice of the professor dictating a text in English. Later, the murmuring of a mysterious chorus reached them, tirelessly repeating the same song over and over again.

It was sunny every day they were there, and Odile and Louis often had lunch with Axter in the Boscombe College dining hall. Axter cooked, set the table, and served the food himself, delighted to be performing these domestic tasks while his wife was away, spending some time in London. Boscombe was the country house of his parents, now deceased, and when he went down from Cambridge he turned the villa into a college, the only way he could keep the house, which had so many childhood memories for him.

Where had he met Bejardy? Oh, it was purely by chance, on a trip to France when he was twenty-five. An American friend had introduced him to "Roland," who was running a floating restaurant on a boat in the Seine, in Neuilly. It's true. It certainly was funny, this "boat-restaurant." But Louis noticed a certain awkwardness in Axter whenever Bejardy was brought up.

In the afternoons, he and Odile would go out and walk down the avenue of Boscombe College, lined with white-fenced houses and bushes so dark green they were almost black. Here and there a pine tree. They would stroll to Fisherman's Walk, an intersection with several stores around it. There was a teashop there, with a high ceiling, large plate-glass windows, and tables so tiny they looked lost in an orangery. At the end of a sloping street was the sea.

A telephone booth, red and solitary, stood in the middle of a roundabout overlooking the beach, and inside it you stood on a carpet of sand several centimeters thick, but the phone worked and the phone book was current. One afternoon, Louis called Brossier collect. He had to give the operator the phone booth's number and they would call him back within half an hour. When the phone rang in the empty landscape, Louis and Odile jumped. A woman's voice: Jacqueline Boivin, Brossier's fiancée.

"Here's Jean-Claude."

Louis asked Brossier how long they had to stay at Bournemouth. Until next week, Brossier said. He was getting ready for his own holidays, with Jacqueline. Where? At Cité Universitaire, of course, in the Deutsch de la Meurthe area. That was better than all the spas and resorts in Europe.

There were dunes with patches of grass growing on the sides. On the peak of these dunes there is sometimes a bench. They leave their clothes on one of these benches and put on the striped bathrobes Axter has lent them. They run down into the sea. The water is icy but they've won their bet: Axter had dared them to swim in the ocean in Bournemouth in April.

They climb back up to the road to Fisherman's Walk, their two robes rolled up in a beach bag. The wind is blowing hard. They enter the teashop the size of an orangery to have a cup of grog.

What if they did stay here several months? Axter would find them a little hotel, or maybe he would continue to put them up. They had forgotten all about about Paris. And it made them happy to hear a foreign language at the tables next to theirs, one they would soon know, soon speak with each other, with the feeling of starting a new life.

At the end of the Boscombe dune road, they met a man in a navy blue raincoat, wearing a checked cap. The man said a few words to them, but they didn't understand what he said very well. He asked them if they were "French students." When they said yes, he waved an ID card with a purple line through it in front of them and said slowly, several times, the words "cinema detective," no doubt trying to convey his profession. Then he offered them a dozen tickets. Free seats, for several movies. They didn't have time to thank him—he was already gone, with his raincoat, too big for him, waving in the wind like a banner.

The cinema was in Christchurch, a neighborhood of Bournemouth near Boscombe College, and the show started every night at nine thirty. They crossed the bridge over the

Stour, a river running between meadows where the grass took on a bluish tint in the twilight. On the other side, a riverside park with a bandstand, shooting galleries, stalls with rows of slot machines, and little refreshment stands on floating decks where boats were moored that you could rent during the day.

Later, this park with its attractions, the river, the sound of the slot machines would be associated in Louis's memory with Odile's smell of lavender—she had found a bottle of perfume at the back of the closet in their room at Boscombe College. A loudspeaker was playing songs and instrumentals. Crowded around the rowboats were groups of men in black leather jackets, who were called "teddy boys." You could hear their arguments and laughter even before you had crossed the bridge.

A girl, also wearing a black leather jacket, would be sitting alone at a table in front of the main refreshment stand, half in shadow. She was a redhead with an upturned Irish nose, her neck adorned with a large chain strung with twenty or more charms. One night, she showed these mementos to Odile and Louis: Each was engraved with a name—Jean-Pierre, Christian, Claude, Bernard, Michel... They had belonged to the French boys she had loved in Bournemouth, at night, under the pier. The others, the teddy boys, avoided her like the plague and never spoke a word to her. But was it her fault she liked Frenchmen?

When they entered the theater, the man in the blue raincoat was standing stiffly next to the cash register. He led them to their seats personally, flashlight in hand. There were never many people in the audience, on the dark brown wooden seats.

While the film was showing, the man walked up and down the center aisle, always in his cap. He sat down every once in a while, and looked around, at a different place each time. At the end of the movie, he would station himself at the cash register again and stare hard at the spectators, one by one, nodding a greeting to Odile and Louis. This was when they should have asked him about his work as a "cinema detective," but his serious, concerned look intimidated them. Louis even felt he should give the man a present in return, to thank him for the free tickets.

They asked Axter what "cinema detective" might mean. Axter had no idea—this was the first time in his life he had heard of such a profession.

When they got back to Boscombe College, the large ground-floor window was often still lit. One night, when they were starting up the stairs, Axter, who had seen them walking across the lawn, waved them over and invited them in for a drink.

They walked into a spacious lounge filled with leather sofas and armchairs, their footsteps sinking into the wool carpet. There were paintings of hunting scenes on the walls, and an engraving that Louis particularly noticed: the members of a family standing around a horse-drawn carriage with a melancholy young man inside. The scene was labeled: *Going Off to College.*

"My wife," Axter said.

A large, sturdy blonde with a severe face and blue eyes, who looked much older than Axter. She was sitting with another woman on one of the sofas.

"Louis and Odile Memling."

Axter had always pretended to believe that they were brother and sister.

"*Enchantée*," she said.

She smiled distractedly at them.

"And this is the wife of my friend Harold Howard."

She hardly looked at them. She was as tall as Mrs. Axter, with very short brown hair and a square, mannish face. She kept shoving a cigarette holder between her teeth with a jerky gesture. The two women continued their conversation without paying any further attention to Odile and Louis. Axter, embarrassed by their cold reception, coughed slightly. Louis, to save face, admired the engraving.

"It's lovely."

"But sad too, don't you think?" Axter said. "Leaving for college. Can you believe I sometimes still have dreams about going off to college. At my age, you understand . . ."

"Michel is a damned sentimentalist," a voice behind them said in nearly perfect French.

They had not heard anyone come in and all three of them turned around.

"May I introduce my friend, Harold Howard."

He was a colossal redhead with age spots on his face, in a dark red turtleneck sweater, a thick tweed jacket, and wide, green velvet trousers.

"Howard is an old friend from Trinity College."

Axter took them over to the part of the lounge as far away as possible from where the two women were talking.

Howard sat down in an armchair and rested his long legs on a windowsill.

Axter leaned toward him. "Guy Burgess sent a postcard," he said, in French, in a low voice.

"Guy? No! Impossible!" Howard said, dumbfounded.

Axter glanced furtively in the direction of the two women, as though needing to keep this important event a secret from them. Then he took the postcard out of his inside jacket pocket and handed it to Howard, who stared at it for a long time, clearly shaken.

"*Wonderful old boy!* He must be unhappy there."

"You know perfectly well that Guy always wanted to be unhappy," Axter said.

Still feeling the shock of the news, Howard mechanically handed the postcard to Louis. It showed a public park in Moscow, and on the back, these simple words:

> With kind regards
> from
> GUY

Louis handed the postcard to Axter, who tucked it back into his pocket. Many years later, at Sunny Home, Louis read about the adventures of Burgess and his friends, and that name, Guy Burgess, was enough to bring back the whole atmosphere of Bournemouth, the rhododendrons, the Boscombe beach, the cool freshness of the ivy, the "cinema detective," Odile's lavender perfume.

"Let's have a drink, to Guy," Axter declared. "*What's your poison?*"

"That means 'What would you like to drink?,'" Howard said.

But Axter was already pouring a drink into their tiny glasses without waiting for an answer: a liquor glinting a dark red that matched Harold Howard's sweater.

"To Guy!" Axter said gravely.

"To Guy!" Odile repeated, laughing.

"To good old Guy!" Harold said.

They drank.

"Guy was the oldest in our group at Dartmouth and Cambridge," Axter said.

Harold looked at Odile and Louis with an engaging smile.

"And what do you do?"

"Not much," Louis said.

"They're still too young to have done anything bad in life," Axter said.

Odile laughed. "Or anything good."

Axter and Howard, in an almost perfectly synchronized gesture, had taken their pipes out of their pockets. Axter stuffed his pipe while Harold didn't take his eyes off Odile and Louis.

"Yes, that's true," Axter said dreamily. "You're both still children . . ."

The lamps cast a harsh light on Odile and Louis, and they moved very close to each other on the sofa. Axter and Harold watched them. Two motionless butterflies, pinned to a piece of cloth, observed by amateur butterfly collectors.

Meanwhile, Harold and Axter had put their pipes in their mouths. The women's whispers from the other end of the lounge were barely audible. Maybe the men were taking advantage of their wives' distance to relax and get comfortable, feel the way they had felt back in their rooms at Trinity College. Axter had unbuttoned the collar of his shirt and draped his calves over one of the arms of the chair. Harold Howard was still leaning his legs on the window-sill, and his tan wool socks, too large for him, slipped slowly down to his ankles.

"You should really see something of England ... If you want, Michael and I can take you on a drive," Harold said. "Don't you think so, Michael? We could take you to Cambridge, for instance."

"I'd be glad to. But I think they're going back to France."

Yes, they were leaving the day after tomorrow. Louis was seized with a feeling of helplessness. What were they going to do in Paris? He felt the need to confide in these Englishmen, even ask their advice. No one had ever once given him and Odile advice. They were alone in the world.

"Really? You have to leave?" Harold said. And he emptied his pipe by nervously knocking it against the heel of his shoe. "Why do you have to go?"

Louis was struck by the childish deception, but also by the unease and affection in Harold Howard's look. They were in strange contrast with his colossal build, the rough tweed, the velvet corduroy, the acrid smell of pipe that enveloped him.

Axter took them to Southampton in the bus he had used to fetch them. The three of them, sitting in the back of the empty bus, did not speak. Axter pensively smoked his pipe. The weather was overcast and gloomy.

The bus parked on the departure pier in front of the customs hangar. Axter was carrying their bags, which he himself presented to the customs officer. Just when they were leaving to board the *Normania*, he caught Louis by the shoulder.

"Still, you should be careful with Roland. Don't let yourself get caught up. He's a charming man, but also a ... a ..." He tried to find the right word. "A kind of adventurer."

They leaned against the railing and waited for their ship to leave. Axter, standing on the running board of the bus, pipe in his mouth, waved goodbye at them wildly with both arms.

Bejardy and Nicole Haas were waiting for them at Le Havre, at the exit from customs. It was almost eight o'clock and getting dark.

"Did you have a good trip?" Bejardy asked in a dull voice.

Nicole Haas smiled at them, without saying anything. They sat in the backseat of Bejardy's car, with Bejardy at the wheel, Nicole Haas next to him.

He drove fast and seemed nervous. He and Nicole Haas had not exchanged a single word, as though they had just had a fight. Bejardy had turned on the radio, and every so often he turned up the volume more.

"So, Roland, have you decided yet?" Nicole Haas asked.

"I don't know, Coco. Maybe the hotel in Verneuil? What do you think?"

She didn't answer. Bejardy turned back to look at Odile and Louis.

"You must be tired from the trip. It doesn't make sense to drive another three hours. We can spend the night at a hotel ... Unless you'd rather go straight back to Paris?"

Without answering, Louis took Odile's hand and

squeezed it. They both felt that there was nothing to say. Anyway, Bejardy had already turned up the radio again.

They had dinner. Nicole Haas hadn't wanted to eat in the large empty dining room at the inn, and Bejardy had chosen a table near the bar.

She was visibly giving Bejardy the cold shoulder, but she was very friendly to Odile and Louis.

"And Axter? How is he doing?" Bejardy asked.

"What do you think of Axter?" Nicole Haas asked at once, as though she wanted them to answer her question and not Bejardy's.

"He's nice," Louis said. "When you met him, you were running a restaurant on a boat, in Neuilly?"

"Ah. So he told you about that?" Bejardy said, looking embarrassed.

"You owned a boat, Roland?" Nicole Haas said ironically. "You? A boat?"

"No. We set up a restaurant on a boat, with Brossier," Bejardy said. "By Bois de Boulogne."

"And what about the boat?"

"It belonged to the Touring Club de France," Bejardy said, getting exasperated.

"I would have loved to see you on that boat. Did you wear a captain's hat?"

And Nicole lit a cigarette with the same nonchalant gesture as that first time in Paris, with the same Zippo lighter that had so surprised Louis.

"Axter is a real Englishman," she said. "Did you see his wife too?"

"Yes."

"She seems more like his mother, don't you think?"

"And yet they're the same age," Bejardy said dryly.

"I don't think so. There must be as big an age difference between them as between you and me."

Bejardy shrugged. He was having trouble keeping his temper. Odile looked back and forth between Bejardy and Nicole, interested in what was happening.

"Doesn't he seem much older than me?" Nicole asked Odile, indicating Bejardy.

Odile didn't know what to say. Louis lowered his head.

"No, I don't think so," Odile said timidly.

"She's polite at least," Nicole said. "And well brought up."

"Much better brought up than you, Coco," Bejardy said.

His face was calm and relaxed again and he had taken Nicole's hand. Underneath it all, Louis thought, Bejardy liked it that Nicole treated him so badly in front of other people. Was it just one of their little games?

"I have never met anyone with a character as bad as Coco's," Bejardy said, stroking her hand.

Louis looked at the Zippo lighter that Nicole had put on the table. He picked it up, lit it, and contemplated the black smoke that the flame gave off.

"When I was in boarding school, I dreamed of having a lighter like this."

"Really?" Nicole said. "You can have it."

She smiled at him and her smile was so sweet, so understanding, that Louis had the feeling their faces could have come closer and closer at that moment, their lips could touch.

"Yes, please. The lighter is yours."

———

Two rooms had been reserved for the night in an annex to the inn, on the other side of the garden. Just as they left the bar, Bejardy took Louis's arm and held him back.

"I wanted to thank you for what you've done for me. We'll discuss it in Paris. You know your commission is waiting for you there, Louis."

"Oh, it was nothing. Really."

In fact, he would have been relieved if Bejardy forgot to give him this commission.

"I insist. You need some pocket money. At your age . . ."

They rejoined Odile and Nicole Haas, who had already crossed the lawn. The path was lit by a lantern hanging on the outside of the annex.

An outdoor staircase led to the second floor, and the rooms opened out onto a balcony with a rough-hewn wooden railing.

"Good night."

"Good night."

Their rooms were next door to each other.

Around two in the morning, Louis and Odile were woken by voices—Bejardy's and Nicole's. At first they couldn't understand what the voices were saying. Bejardy was talking nonstop and it seemed to Louis that he was reading something or talking to someone on the phone.

"You bastard!" Nicole Haas shouted.

"Shut up!"

Something shattered on the floor.

"You're crazy! You'll wake everyone up!"

"I don't care!"

"Do you think they'll start hitting each other?" Odile said.

She leaned her head against the hollow of Louis's shoulder. They didn't move.

"You can keep your dough!" Nicole Haas shouted. "I'm taking the car and going back to Paris!"

"Enough already!"

One of them slapped the other. The sound of a scuffle.

"Crook! Crook! You're just a pathetic crook!"

"Shut up!"

"Murderer!!"

"Coco…"

He must have covered her mouth with his hand, because her voice sounded muffled, like a moan.

"Bastard! Bastard!"

"All right, calm down. Calm down, Coco."

Their voices got softer. Suddenly, they laughed. Silence. She let out a sigh, then another, at intervals that grew closer and closer together.

Odile and Louis stayed motionless, their eyes wide. A latticework of reflections played on the blanket.

"I wonder what's happening over there," Louis said.

After a few moments, he felt the same smothering feeling of dependence in this room that he had felt in boarding school and in the army. The days followed one another and you wondered what was happening over there, and you hardly believed that you would ever be free of this prison.

"We have to leave," Odile said.

Leave. Of course. Bejardy had no hold over him. None at all. He didn't owe him anything. No one and nothing had any hold over him. Even the school yard and the barracks yard now seemed unreal to him, and harmless, like the memory of a little park somewhere.

BROSSIER was waiting for them at one of the outdoor tables at place Jussieu, since the night was warm. When Odile and Louis arrived, he stood up and gave them a hug, a gesture full of an affection that was unusual for him.

He had changed a lot since they'd left for England. He was wearing an old sky-blue tracksuit jacket and sneakers, his face was thinner, and he was starting to grow a beard, which he stroked from time to time.

"Louis. I have big news for you. I'm not working with Bejardy any more. It's over."

He waited with a triumphant look for Louis and Odile's reaction.

"What are you going to do now?" Odile asked.

"Listen ... I've never been this happy." He puffed up his chest with pride. "I've signed up at the Faculty of Sciences, as an independent auditor. That'll let me feel even closer to Jacqueline. We're in the same building, Quai Saint-Bernard."

"You've broken with Bejardy completely?" Louis asked.

"Completely. I don't ever want to see him again. I'm making a clean break with that whole period of my life. I'm an entirely different person now, Louis."

Between the traveling salesman with the puffy face Louis had met in Saint-Lô and this man in his tracksuit jacket, with shining eyes and haggard cheeks, there was not the slightest family resemblance. Had he even kept his Tyrolean hats?

"I'm sorry I'm in such a funny outfit," Brossier said. "I've just come from a gym I go to once a week."

"And what about me?" Louis suddenly said. "I'm supposed to stay with Bejardy alone? You're just going to drop me?"

"No, not at all. I hope you'll follow my lead...Jacqueline won't be long, her class runs a little later tonight."

The square with its trees was like one in a country town. There were a few people at the edge of the sidewalk playing boule. Music from a jukebox came out of the café-tabac next door.

"I had to show you this neighborhood. You have the Jardin des Plantes right nearby, and the Arènas de Lutèce, where Jacqueline takes me every now and then. When we don't go to the U restaurant or the cafeteria, we have dinner in a little Mexican place next to the Arènas. Let's all go together some night, if you want."

His voice was no longer gutteral, it was alive with excitement, clear and melodious. He had left his usual vocabulary behind, and the slang words that had always spiced up his conversation before—bones, sharp, zilch, brass nickel—would now have sounded all wrong coming from his mouth.

Jacqueline Boivin came and sat down at their table, and rested a student satchel on her knees. Louis was entranced by her Ethiopian grace.

"How was class?" Brossier asked, kissing her on the forehead.

"Good."

She turned to Odile and Louis.

"It's nice to see you again. Has Jean-Claude told you?" Her face sought their approval.

"I think he's doing the right thing," Louis said.

"Will you walk us to Cité?" Brossier suggested. "We can have a bite to eat there. I'll carry your book bag, Jacqueline."

They passed the Lycée Henri-IV, then the Sainte-Geneviève church, and came out on place du Panthéon, with Jacqueline Boivin on Brossier's arm and he with the satchel in his hand.

"Do you know this area?" Brossier asked.

"No," Odile said. "I've never been to college."

"It's never too late! Here's proof." He pointed to himself and then kissed Jacqueline on the neck.

"All you need to do is fill out the registration forms," Louis said.

On rue Soufflot, by the outdoor tables of the Mahieu, there were groups of people in lively conversation drifting by from left to right. Brossier, not moving, pulled Jacqueline Boivin closer to him. Next to them, Odile and Louis let the clusters of people push past them and were almost carried away in the stream. Luckily, Brossier held them firmly by the hand.

"On the right," he said, in a tour guide's sententious voice, "on boulevard Saint-Michel, you have Capoulade... Then the Picart bookstore, where I often go with Jacqueline. And Chanteclair, the record store... Farther down, there's Gibert, where I sometimes sell used books to get a little pocket money. And the Café de Cluny. There's a pool table on the second floor..."

He sounded breathless, as though panicking at the

thought that there wasn't enough time to introduce them to all the many delights of the neighborhood. A whole life wouldn't be enough time.

At the Gare du Luxembourg they waited on benches for the Sceaux line train to arrive.

"You need to follow my lead, Louis, and make a clean break with Roland. I'm sure you can influence him, Odile. He doesn't need to work for Bejardy."

In the train bringing them to Cité Universitaire, Brossier affectionately held Jacqueline Boivin against his shoulder.

"Let me speak frankly with you, Louis. Roland is a desperate man. Don't stay on a sinking ship."

"Have you known him a long time?" Louis asked.

He felt that now he could ask the questions Brossier had always answered vaguely before, and that this time, now that it was over between him and Bejardy, Brossier would explain everything, down to the last detail.

"I met Bejardy right after the war. Almost twenty years ago now…"

"That was when you ran a restaurant together, on a boat?" Louis said.

"Ah, yes. The Longchamp Schooner. Who told you about that? It was a real disaster. Roland wanted the waiters to wear Provençal cowboy outfits."

He gave Jacqueline a mischievous kiss on the cheek.

"You're not bored with these old war stories, are you, darling?"

Jacqueline kindly shrugged her shoulders and gave Odile a complicitous glance. They had reached the Denfert-Rochereau station.

"I met Roland when I was eighteen. He was five years older than me."

He leaned toward Louis.

"Roland's problem can be captured in a single sentence: 'I want to, but I can't.' Let me put it more crudely, if you don't mind: Roland always farted louder than his ass."

Now this was the Brossier from Saint-Lô.

They got out at the Cité Universitaire station. A boy nearby was kicking a soccer ball and Brossier made a fake and managed to dribble the ball all the way to the stairs without the boy being able to get it back. He was over the moon at his accomplishment.

"Should we have a bite at the Turk's place?" Brossier said. "It's a little farther down."

They walked down boulevard Jourdan toward Charléty Stadium. Pink and blue neon lit up a kind of glassed-in counter in the middle of the sidewalk, under the trees, with a few tables around it.

"Four club sandwiches and four pints of the blonde on tap," Brossier ordered.

The wind carried the smells of Parc Montsouris over to them, and the night was bright enough for them to see the palace of the Bey of Tunis on the great lawn. Opposite them, on the other side of the empty street, was the Great Britain building, whose wood-paneled dining hall Brossier had said he liked. An empty bus appeared from time to time at the station a little farther up.

"What are you two doing for the holidays?" Brossier asked.

He and Jacqueline had decided to stay in Paris during July and August. In the mornings they would sunbathe on the Cité Universitaire lawns. In the afternoons, they'd play tourist—go visit Les Invalides, the Louvre, the Eiffel Tower, Sainte-Chapelle. At night, they'd have dinner on a bateau mouche. Maybe they'd venture out as far as Versailles, on a tour bus for "organized visits," and "catch a sound and light show" at the Bassin de Neptune fountain.

"I love doing that kind of thing as a vacation," Jacqueline said. "You should come with us."

"The main thing," Brossier said, "is to always go on group tours. Everything completely taken care of. With guides. You understand, Louis. Guides."

He insisted on that. For a long time, he had felt an urgent need for "organization," for "guides."

But Louis was set on finding out how Brossier had met Bejardy.

"To begin at the beginning," Brossier said, "I met Roland right after the war, at a family pension in Neuilly called the Chestnut Trees. He was living there with his mother and his fiancée at the time, an Englishwoman."

And he, Jean-Claude Brossier, a fat young man of nineteen, got off the boat in Normandy and enrolled in the art school in Paris, École Boulle. But he soon forgot about art school and joined in the rhythm of their lives. They took drives around the countryside, sometimes as far as Deauville; went to the races; played bridge at night with Bejardy's mother in the little living room at the Chestnut Trees. Roland had earned a Médaille militaire in Germany and was going into business. And Hélène, Roland's fiancée... She was so lazy. One day, when a bag of coffee turned up at the pension—something rare in that period of rationing—Hélène had let out a sigh at the prospect of having to grind the beans.

Jacqueline Boivin chewed quietly on her sandwich. Odile had a cigarette at her lips, which Louis lit with the

Zippo. And Brossier? He seemed sad, all of a sudden, from bringing up these distant memories. His face was drawn, and Louis was sorry he had asked him these questions.

"It's true, I came here from Normandy to go to art school."

He looked paler and paler, as though realizing that the satchel he had on his knees, his tracksuit jacket and student status, even Jacqueline herself with her gray pleated skirt and beige twinset, were no longer enough to protect him from the passage of time and the indifference of the world.

Louis started working again, as a watchman in the garage on rue Delaizement, mornings and afternoons. Or else he took letters to addresses in Paris and on the outskirts, the same as he'd done before leaving for England.

He had refused his commission, despite Bejardy's insistence, and when Bejardy told him, in a voice of feigned indifference, that the movers were coming to take the furniture and the files out of the garage, Louis could sense disaster in the air, but he didn't dare ask any questions.

"I'm liquidating the garage," Bejardy told him.

It was already empty. The American cars had disappeared, the Mercedes too. The only car left was an old gray Simca with flat tires, all the way in the back, but it had never once moved from its place.

One afternoon, Louis helped Bejardy move the files down to where a brick chimney ran up the wall, next to the Simca. Bejardy put a couple of logs in the fireplace, opened the file folders, threw the pages into the fire one by one, and stirred the ashes with a long iron poker.

"Fire purifies everything," he said, lost in thought.

"So, Brossier isn't working with us anymore?" Louis asked.

"How do you know?"

"I saw him the other day."

Bejardy, sitting on the running board of the Simca, studied one of the files. He raised his head.

"I think he's in love. What can I do about that?"

"He told me he's known you a long time . . ."

"Yes, we're old friends, almost since childhood," Bejardy said in an evasive tone.

"You met each other right after the war, in a family pension in Neuilly?"

A nervous look passed over Bejardy's face.

"What else did he tell you?"

"Nothing. That you lived there with your mother."

"I see. He told you about my mother?"

A hint of a smile. Then his face clouded over again.

"I've spent my whole life dragging Brossier behind me. Slowing me down. It often happens that way, you know, things like that."

He stood up and went over to the fireplace to throw several pages in.

"He told me he wants to try to live his own life now, Louis." And he let out a short laugh, more like a cough. "The only problem is, he's too old. One day he'll come looking for me again, with his tail between his legs, I'm sure of it. But by then I'll be gone . . ."

Rays of sunlight shone through the windows in back, making a large patch of light on the floor. Louis and Bejardy stayed sitting in the middle of this patch, like hikers stopping for a moment in a clearing. The fire crackled.

"I'm liquidating my affairs here," Bejardy said. "But I need you to do one last thing for me, my dear Louis."

He came out of a cross street onto Quai Louis-Blériot and walked into the building, the green shopping bag in his hand. Bejardy opened the door for him.

"You're sure you have all the rest of the files?"

"Yes."

Bejardy quickly looked through the folders stuffed in the bag.

"Give them here."

He walked ahead of Louis. From behind, with the shopping bag, he had a strange silhouette, like someone coming back from the market.

In the living room, Louis saw that the furniture was gone. There was nothing left but the large sofa and two chairs. The bookshelves had been emptied out, too, and the books were stacked in piles against the wall.

"I'm going to liquidate the apartment," Bejardy said. "If you're interested in any of these books..."

They went over to the sofa. Nicole Haas, in riding pants, was lying there asleep. Her cheek was pressed against the arm of the sofa, and Louis was moved by the relaxed face, the slightly open mouth. Bejardy tapped her softly on the shoulder. She opened her eyes and sat up when she saw Louis.

"Sorry..."

"Nothing to worry about, darling."

The wind was billowing the gauze curtains through the open French windows, the same as on the day when Odile and Louis had met Nicole Haas for the first time.

"You should make the most of the nice weather, Coco," Bejardy said. "What are you doing this afternoon?"

"I need to go see the horses."

"Louis can take you in the car. I need to stay here. I have some work to do."

The telephone rang and Bejardy went to the other end of the room to answer it. Louis sat down facing Nicole Haas. She didn't say anything but she smiled at him, her face still a bit sleepy. And that smile, those bright eyes fixed on him, the dreamlike undulation of the curtains in the wind, the sound of a boat's motor—it all made up one of the moments that remained in his memory.

On rue de la Ferme, in Neuilly, she told him to stop in front of a low building with a bar that filled the whole ground floor: the Lauby. Wood walls. Semidarkness. Photographs of horses and riders. Stirrups. Whips. The smell of leather.

A man at one of the tables stood up and came over to kiss Nicole Haas's hand. He was in riding clothes too: a small man, very stiff, with black hair and a black mustache, looking a bit like a wax dummy. The words got scrambled in his mouth—this syllable delayed, that one swallowed, the next stammered—and he imitated the halting pronunciation of certain Anglo-Saxons so perfectly that you ended up wondering if he was even speaking French. Nicole Haas told Louis that this man was a marquis, and that during a long stay in America he had married a movie actress and become her "manager." On returning to France, he had taken over the stables across the street from the Lauby. The only thing he had brought back from America was the title of "manager," which now appeared on his calling cards and which he valued more than his title of nobility.

"So, you're leaving your horses for a while again, Nicole?"

"Yes. Another month."

"And then Argentina? It's decided? Tell me."

"I don't know."

"You must tell me before you go. I have very good friends there. Dodero, Gracida...Pierre Eyzaguirre...No, he's Chilean. One can never tell them apart, all those gauchos."

The marquis's voice had taken on a very shrill tone when he said his friends' names.

"Something to drink? Would you like one? Scotch? Coffee? Tea? Tell me."

He twirled his hands in strange circles, as though his shirt cuffs were bothering him.

"Do you ride?"

"No," Louis said.

"Why not?"

"He hasn't had free time to learn yet," Nicole Haas said.

"You simply must start," the marquis said gravely.

They left the Lauby and walked through the stable gates.

"I will leave you here," the marquis said. "I have to give a riding lesson to Robert de Unzue's daughter. See you very soon, Nicole. And be sure to tell me about Argentina, yes? I also need to know so I can take care of the horses..."

The marquis waved goodbye with an abrupt movement of his hand, and they crossed the sand-covered courtyard to the stables. Nicole Haas wanted to show Louis her horses. She had two, a dappled gray and a bay. They stuck their heads out of their stalls and she stroked their heads.

Above the stables there was a kind of dovecote covered with ivy.

"I have a room up there. Do you want to see it?"

They climbed a tiny spiral staircase. Nicole Haas opened the door to a little room wallpapered with toile de Jouy, with a narrow bed covered with pale blue velvet.

"I come here a lot. It's the only place where I feel good. I'm near the horses."

She opened the window halfway, then lay down on the bed.

"I always wondered why you work with Roland."

"Just one of those things," Louis said.

He sat down on the floor with his back against the side of the bed.

"And what are you going to do when he leaves?"

"I don't know," Louis said. "What about you?"

"Whether it's him or someone else, what matters is that I find someone who will let me feed my horses."

She pressed her kind and stubborn face into the hollow of Louis's shoulder.

"He wants to take me to Argentina. What am I supposed to do in Argentina?"

He felt her breath on his neck.

"Did you know that Roland is a murderer? That's right, a murderer...There were articles in the paper. Why am I going to Argentina with a murderer? You don't seem to understand what I'm saying, Louis. Me, all alone down there with that killer..."

How long did they stay there in that room, on the narrow bed? She had a scar on her shoulder, in the shape of a star, that Louis couldn't help but run his lips over. A souvenir of a fall from a horse. It got dark. They could hear the clattering of hooves, a whinny, and the high-pitched voice of the marquis giving orders at more and more distant intervals, like a motif on a flute, clear and desolate, returning again and again.

WE WERE slipping toward summer. Bejardy had less and less work for Louis, who spent most of his days with Odile. They met Brossier and Jacqueline Boivin at Cité Universitaire sometimes, and picnicked on the great lawn or strolled to Parc Montsouris. More often, Mary came to Montmartre. She had discovered a little place, "lease for sale," for her "Couture Fashion" boutique.

At night, they walked slowly along the median to place Blanche and Pigalle. They went to see Jordan, who had managed to get a gig in a cabaret on rue des Martyrs and who always wore the stage dress Odile and Mary had made. Or else they simply went up rue Caulaincourt to avenue Junot and then back the way they had come. The lights were on all night in the entrance to the Hotel Rome on rue Caulaincourt, like a lookout post.

On avenue Junot, they saw a big man walking an Irish setter on a leash, and nodded a greeting. The dog seemed to feel a spontaneous affection for Odile and Louis.

That night, on the terrace of the Dream, this same man was sitting at a table next to theirs and his Irish setter had put its chin on Odile's knee.

"My dog isn't bothering you, is he, mademoiselle? If he is, please don't hesitate to tell him."

He hardly moved his lips, but his bass voice carried far.

"No, he's not bothering me at all," Odile said, petting the dog.

"Do you live in the neighborhood?"

"Yes," Louis said. "A little farther down, on this street."

"What building?"

"Eighteen bis."

"Which floor?"

Louis hesitated a moment before answering. "The sixth."

"No, impossible! In the studio?"

"Yes."

"May I?"

He moved over to join Odile and Louis, clearly deeply moved. His short gray hair, his puffy face, his powerful brow, and his build, emphasized by his velvet courduroy jacket, made him look like a former boxer. He gave off a smell of old leather and cold ashes.

"That used to be my studio. Can you believe it?"

There was something about him, although they couldn't quite put their finger on what, that contradicted the big, brutal features of his face.

"You have to admit, sometimes very strange coincidences happen in life..."

"Are you a painter?" Odile asked, continuing to pet the dog.

"I was, yes. When I lived in the studio. I drew covers for music-hall programs. But I'm not going to tell you my life story. By the way, did you keep the bar and the fan?"

"Yes," Louis said.

"The Chinese drawings are mine."

He looked at Odile and Louis with his sensitive eyes, head raised, a slightly ironic smile on his lips.

"I haven't introduced myself. Bauer. Let me invite you

over to my place for a plum schnaps, to celebrate this strange coincidence. It's right nearby."

His voice was so commanding that they truly had no choice but to accept.

On avenue Junot, they walked through the entrance arch of one those little buildings built in the thirties, with bay windows and arcades. Bauer and the dog preceded them.

"Would you mind keeping as quiet as you can?" he said in his deep voice. "My mother is sleeping."

They walked down the hall on tiptoe and into an enormous room, either a living room or dining room. Bauer quietly shut the door behind them.

"Now we can talk. My mother won't hear anything while we're in here."

The room was furnished with a sideboard, a table, and rustic-style walnut-colored chairs. A Tyrolean pendulum clock on the wall between the two windows, an armchair upholstered in cream-colored silk, and some roses in a vase on the shelf of the sideboard made the decor a little more cheerful. Louis noticed a photograph, taken into the light, of a man leaning against the mast of a sailboat, his silhouette sharp against the background of a glittering sea.

"Alain Gerbault...I knew him well when I was seventeen," Bauer said.

That photo gave a nostalgic charm to the room, like a breath of fresh air from the open sea or the sound of a Hawaiian ukelele.

"Have a seat. Please, sit down."

The table was covered with an oilskin cloth. The dog climbed up onto a chair next to Odile and stayed there, alert, not letting Bauer out of his sight while he poured some plum schnaps into champagne flutes for them.

"Your dog looks like he wants some too!" Odile said.

Bauer laughed. "All right. Why not? A glass for the dog."

He filled another flute right to the rim and pushed it toward the suspicious dog. Then he took a large green leather album out of one of the sideboard drawers.

"Here you go. Souvenirs from back when I lived in the studio. Where you live now."

Louis had opened the album and Bauer stayed standing behind him and Odile and the dog. The first two pages had a single photograph each, protected by a sheet of clear plastic. Two men with regular features, one dark and the other blond. The photos were from the thirties.

"Pierre Meyer and van Duren. Two music-hall artists," Bauer said. "The two men I admired more than anyone else in my life."

"Why?" Odile asked.

"Because they were beautiful," Bauer said in a peremptory tone. "They committed suicide, both of them. Alain Gerbault too, in a way."

Louis turned the album's pages. There were covers of various music-hall programs signed "Bauer" in a large, slashing hand.

"You didn't know my mother, by any chance, did you?" Louis asked. "She worked at the Tabarin."

"Your mother? No, my boy. I didn't know anyone at the Tabarin. I usually worked for Mistinguett."

There were photos on the following pages of young people, with their names and dates getting closer and closer to the present. The generations passed, one after the other, and in the middle of all these young people, each more dazzling than the last, was an older man with an ordinary, fat face, sinuous lips, and wrinkles around his eyes.

"That's Tonton, from Liberty's."

The harsh light from the hanging lamp was reflected as gleams from the sheets of plastic covering all the mementos. The dog seemed interested in the album, too: He sniffed and snorted from time to time, and his breath clouded up the photographs whenever Louis didn't turn the page in time. Odile leaned her head on Louis's shoulder to see better.

"They're fascinating, your photos," she said. "Do you look at them often?"

"No. They depress me."

"Why?"

"It's sad to think about all those beautiful boys, all old now, or dead. And I'm still here, like a rotting old hulk that has seen them all come and go. Nothing's left but their photos. I wanted to make another album, of all the dogs I've had in my life, but I don't have the strength."

His voice was hoarse. He let himself sink into a chair and took Odile's hand.

"You're still too young to understand, my dear. But when I look through this album and see them, one after the other, I have a feeling of waves, approaching and breaking, then another, then another..."

Louis was stunned. He couldn't believe his eyes. Under the shining plastic sheet was a photo of Brossier and Bejardy, next to each other, Brossier's face round and still partly a child's, Bejardy barely twenty-five, with wavy black hair and the face and smile of a charmer.

"Did you know them?" Louis asked, wiping off the condensation that the dog's breath had left on the plastic.

Bauer pulled the album onto his lap for a look.

"Yes, yes...The short one, there, who looks like Roland Toutain, I told him to go take an acting class." His finger was pointing to Brossier. "Nothing came of it. I even got him a job working with me at an antique shop. Later, I think he became a flight attendant. Air Brazzaville. The other one, that's different. He tried to sell me paintings... He turned out badly. He went on trial for killing an American. Acquitted. I kept the articles from the papers, if you're interested... He ended up running a restaurant on a boat, in Neuilly. Even wanted me to do the decorations, something 'pirate-themed.' Do you want the press clippings about him?"

"Sure, thank you," Louis said, pretending it didn't much matter to him.

Slipping a hand under the photograph, Bauer pulled out an envelope and handed it to Louis, who slipped it into his pocket right away, as though it were a bag of cocaine.

"I'm so glad these things of the past still interest you," Bauer said.

"Where did you meet them?" Odile asked, stunned.

"Meet them? I don't know anymore. At Tonton's place, maybe. I'm losing my memory... All right, children, that's enough for now."

He abruptly closed the album and put it back in the sideboard drawer.

"If you're good, I'll give you that album someday."

Louis stood up, in a state of great confusion. He stood stock-still, dazed by his discovery.

"Allow me," Bauer said, making a sign for him to sit back down.

He had a camera in his hand and was attaching a tiny flash.

"I just bought it. You can get a color photo instantly… Move closer, you two. Guy, you too."

Louis turned around, and Bauer smiled.

"Guy is my dog."

Guy pressed his muzzle into Odile's wrist. Bauer looked through the viewfinder.

"Very nice. I'll get all three of you."

The flash made Louis blink. He thought about Bejardy and Brossier. But he also repeated in his mind Bauer's little phrase: "waves, approaching and breaking, then another, then another…" No doubt Bauer would stick their photo in his album, with the date, and then Odile and he and the dog would have been nothing but one wave coming after all the others.

The envelope contained a yellowed newspaper clipping:

In a family pension in Neuilly, rue Charles-Lafitte, federal police investigators last night arrested Roland Chantain de Bejardy, age 25, the alleged murderer of the American, Parker.

It is now known that Parker, who came to France in early 1946, had had serious trouble with the law in his own country. An inquiry has been opened in France into the trafficking in surplus American products Parker organized with an accomplice working for the Saint-Cloud post exchange. Tractors, tarpaulins, and radio equipment were among the items in question, and Chantain de Bejardy was one of the men assigned by Howard Parker to dispose of the merchandise.

The young man apparently acted as a private secretary for Parker, who was around twenty years older. According to some witnesses, they were often seen together at the Stage on rue Pierre-Charron, a bar where Parker used to meet people. They were seen together at the Stage a few hours before the murder.

Roland Chantain de Bejardy, from an excellent family, claims to be an art dealer. At the Liberation, he was serving in de Lattre's army, where his heroic conduct earned him the Médaille militaire at age twenty-three. His father was known in equestrian circles and was a longtime president of Tattersalls in France and the Biarritz Polo Club. The family ran into difficulties upon his death, and Chantain de Bejardy lived with his mother in the pension in Neuilly where he was arrested.

Two of his close friends, Hélène Mitford and Jean-Claude Brossier, age nineteen, who likewise lived at the pension on rue Charles-Lafitte, have been questioned by the federal police. The evidence against Chantain seems overwhelming, and enabled the authorities to identify him within forty-eight hours. First, the testimony of Jean Tolle, a garageman from Meriel, who saw the murderer and gave the authorities a detailed description: He was approximately twenty-five years old, tall, and very elegant. The man in question bought two containers of gasoline from Monsieur Tolle. Madame Seck, living in Garches, also gave a description of the murderer, which matched Tolle's. She was walking her dogs in the woods, heading toward Rueil, when she heard two shots fired quickly. A car started and drove by her a few yards away, so close that she had time to see the driver: a man about twenty-five years old, like the one who had bought gas in Meriel, and like him with black hair and delicate features, clean-shaven. A man was collapsed next to him, leaning on his shoulder. Something seemed wrong, and Madame Seck wrote down the license plate number, 9092 RM: the dark red Delahaye 12 CV that Chantain de Bejardy drove and which was often seen parked in front of the Neuilly pension.

At first, it was hard to explain what might have led Chantain de Bejardy to murder Parker. Maybe it was a disagreement between them about something to do with their trafficking operation.

Stuck to the back of the article was a newspaper headline:

CHANTAIN DE BEJARDY
ACQUITTED—REASONABLE DOUBT
His colonel and one of his old comrades in the
1st French Army testified on his behalf

The word "DOUBT" was double-underlined in red and three exclamation points were written next to it in the same red ink, in nervous handwriting, hard enough to puncture the paper. The handwriting was clearly Bauer's.

He ended up deciding on Paris-Nord, a large brasserie with a brown façade on rue de Dunkerque. Louis and Odile walked in behind him.

Bejardy seemed to know the place and he led them to a table in the back, where a frosted-glass wall let in daylight filtered pale green. The room was empty. They could see a corner of Gare du Nord from where they sat.

Bejardy looked at his watch. "Twenty more minutes..."

He had no luggage except for a leather bag and a brief-case, which he put on a seat next to him.

"We'll meet in Geneva the day after tomorrow at ten a.m. sharp, in the lobby of the Richmond Hotel. Here are the two round-trip tickets to Annecy. I checked, there's a bus from Annecy to Geneva at five o'clock. Since the train gets into Annecy around three, that will leave you two hours free."

He turned to Odile: "Do you mind taking this trip?"

"Not at all."

"This is the last thing you'll do for me. Here."

He put the briefcase on Louis's lap.

"The same as what you took to Axter, more or less. This time, I insist you take a commission, old boy. We'll discuss it again in Geneva. Yes, yes, I insist... On the bus, you'll need to be discreet about hiding the money. This looks a little fancy, doesn't it," he said, indicating the briefcase.

"Don't worry," Louis said.

"I have to take a quick trip to Brussels. Arrange some things there. That'll burn the last bridge. Then, Argentina."

He rubbed his palms as though playing the cymbals.

"Why Argentina?" Louis asked.

"I have family there, on my mother's side. And Nicole can spend time with her horses...Oh, I just thought of something. If you need to reach me tomorrow, call the Métropole in Brussels. Ask for Monsieur Chantain."

He wrote "Chantain" down on the envelope containing the train tickets.

"It's part of my name. Chantain de Bejardy is my name, you see."

Odile and Louis exchanged a look, and Louis was about to show Bejardy the old newspaper clipping. He had it in his hand, in the inside pocket of his jacket, but he changed his mind.

Bejardy's face looked pasty under the light coming through the wall of glass. It was as if he were growing older before their eyes.

"It's strange," he said. "I lived in this neighborhood by Gare du Nord, after I got out of prison."

"You were in prison?"

"I'm joking, old boy. But I did live in this neighborhood for a long time. Boulevard Magenta. It doesn't look like much, but the neighborhood grows on you once you get to know it."

He considered the empty room around him.

"Back then, I used to come here a lot to have dinner with a girl. A blonde. She lived in the neighborhood too. Her name was Geneviève..."

Bejardy's face took on a tired, confused expression.

Maybe because there was nothing left of this Geneviève but a deserted dining room.

"And you? What do you plan to do in the future?" he asked.

"I don't know," Louis said. "Take a vacation."

"How old are you two, exactly?"

"I'll be twenty in three days," Odile said.

"And you, Louis?"

"I'll be twenty in a month and a half."

Bejardy raised his cup, with a pensive look. "Well, here's to your twentieth birthdays!" He gulped down his coffee.

"All right. I have to leave you now. No, no, stay here. I hate goodbyes on train platforms. The day after tomorrow, at the Richmond, ten o'clock on the dot. Goodbye, Madame Memling."

Louis walked him to the brasserie exit anyway, briefcase in hand.

"Don't get caught on the bus to Geneva ... It'll be easy. You look so nice, my dear Louis. I wonder if I looked nice like that, when I was your age. Do you think I did?"

"I don't know," Louis said.

He crossed the street to Gare du Nord and waved his arm without turning back. This slow, vague movement of his arm surprised Louis, and stayed in his memory as a gesture of benediction.

It was still light out, and they wandered at random through the neighborhood where there once had lived Roland Chantain de Bejardy and a blonde named Geneviève. Louis carried the briefcase under his arm. They walked to Gare de l'Est and then turned back near Gare du Nord. It was a part of town that trains left from, with heavy façades, small shops, dusty lawyer's offices, diamond dealers, and brasseries giving off the beery smell of Alsace and Belgium.

They did not know that this was their last walk through Paris. They did not yet exist as individuals at all; they were blended together with the façades and the sidewalks. In macadam roads, the stones, patched together like an old cloth, have dates written on them to indicate when the successive layers of tar have been poured, but perhaps also recording births, encounters, deaths. Later, when they remembered this period in their life, they would see these intersections and building entryways again. They had registered every last ray of light coming off of them, every reflection. They themselves had been nothing but bubbles, iridescent with the city's colors: gray and black.

Place Saint-Vincent-de-Paul, with its square and its church, was as silent and empty as the familiar places you move through in a dream. They went back to the large boulevards via rue d'Hauteville and lost themselves in the crowd by Café Brébant.

Odile fell asleep. He slipped out of bed and tiptoed over to the window. It was raining in Annecy. In the park down below, children were chasing each other under the watchful eye of someone who stayed still; all you could see of him or her was the convex surface of a black umbrella.

Louis had chosen this hotel because it was near the station. Back in boarding school, when he spent his days off in Annecy, he had been curious about its ocher façade. He could still picture in his mind the blond man meandering around the Promenade du Pâquier one Saturday. He was known as "Carlton," from the name of the hotel where he had been a groom in the old days; according to legend, he carried at all times a Browning in a gray buckskin holster against his heart.

Annecy hadn't changed in three years. It was raining, just as on the Sundays when they had to be back at school by seven. There had been nothing to do on those Sundays except take shelter under the arcades of La Taverne or under the awning of the Casino. Or hug the walls and the windows on rue Royale. Later, in Saint-Lô, it was still raining, and you had to step over puddles, and, if you think about it, between the boarding school and the barracks there were nine years of rain and squat toilets you could count on the fingers of one hand.

Louis could see the station from the hotel window. The bus to Geneva would leave from a bright building to the left. One day, he had taken that bus with the friend of his father's who was serving as Louis's tutor. They went through Cruseilles and Saint-Julien. Two customs posts to get through.

On the other side of the station, on Sunday evenings, he would wait for the bus that stopped a hundred yards from the boarding school. It was always full and you had to stay standing the whole ride. At the bend in the road at Veyrier-du-Lac, the castle of Menthon-Saint-Bernard would appear on the mountaintop like a phantom ship on the crest of a wave. Farther on, at the edge of the road, the little cemetery in Alex...

The briefcase was on the night table. He picked it up and went to sit by the window. He could hear Odile's regular breathing. It was four o'clock. The bus to Geneva left at 5:22.

He opened the briefcase. Rolls of 500-franc bills. New. He looked out at the station across the street.

One Sunday, he had let the bus leave without him and gone back to his "tutor," telling him he had missed it. The "tutor" had driven him back to the boarding school himself, in his Citroën.

But now the years of gray and rain were coming to an end, and to him they seemed so far away already that he could remember them fondly. He started to count the rolls of bills. Yes. The decision had been made.

He woke up Odile. That same night, they took a train to Nice. Connection in Lyon. Ten minutes wait.

They spent two weeks in Nice. They had rented a big American convertible, with which, in the months to follow, they would explore the Côte d'Azur.

One morning, driving along the Corniche between Nice and Villefranche-sur-Mer, Louis felt a curious sensation of both stupor and lightness, and he was curious if Odile felt it too.

Something—he wondered later if it was simply his youth—something that had weighed upon him until that moment broke off him, the way a piece of rock slides slowly into the sea and disappears in a spray of foam.

TITLES IN SERIES

For a complete list of titles, visit www.nyrb.com or write to:
Catalog Requests, NYRB, 435 Hudson Street, New York, NY 10014

* *Also available as an electronic book.*